DATE DUE

Humphrey	TH		
Franklin			
Wester			
Wilkins			
Ferguson			
Fitzhugh			
Brinkley			
Cather			
Bentling			
McDonald			
B. Burden			
C. Griffin			
J. Jenkins			
Sullivan			
Starcher			
Blair			

DEMCO 38-296

The Coin Conspiracy

This Large Print Book carries the
Seal of Approval of N.A.V.H.

The Coin Conspiracy

Church choir mysteries
#9

Eileen M. Berger

Itm 3956
26.95
LT-AF
8/2003

Thorndike Press • Waterville, Maine

Published in 2003 by arrangement with Guideposts Book Division.

Thorndike Press Large Print Christian Mystery Series.

The tree indicium is a trademark of Thorndike Press.

The text of this Large Print edition is unabridged.
Other aspects of the book may vary from the original edition.

Set in 16 pt. Plantin by Al Chase.

Printed in the United States on permanent paper.

Library of Congress Cataloging-in-Publication Data

Berger, Eileen M.
    The coin conspiracy / Eileen M. Berger.
      p. cm. — (Church choir mysteries)
    ISBN 0-7862-4976-5 (lg. print : hc : alk. paper)
    1. Choirs (Music) — Fiction. 2. Large type books.
I. Title. II. Series.
PS3552.E7183C6 2003
  813'.54—dc21   2002043597

*This book is dedicated to all those everywhere
who faithfully and joyously sing in
church choirs —
especially to those with whom
I've participated for years
in the choir of the Hughesville Baptist Church.*

Acknowledgments

Thanks to those special people at Guideposts Book and Inspirational Media Division who make these novels possible by keeping us writers encouraged, even while incorporating those changes and adaptations that make our work better.

I salute you, Elizabeth Kramer Gold, Michele Slung and Stephanie Castillo Samoy! I've appreciated getting to know you by phone and with written words, and hope someday to meet you personally.

And a hearty "bravo" to Brigitte Weeks, editor-in-chief of Guideposts Books. What varied responsibilities you have, and how capably you serve! We are all indebted to you.

1

The outside temperature had officially hit ninety-eight degrees, but nobody had turned on the air conditioning in the sanctuary of Eternal Hope Community Church — this would have been regarded by some as unjustified expense for an under two-hour choir practice. That didn't stop people from griping, however, so Gracie Parks tried to change the subject by asking, "Have any of you been out Ferris Road recently?"

Lester Twomley looked at her and grinned, understanding her diversionary tactics.

She smiled, realizing he knew exactly what she was doing, then she sobered again. "Gooseberry and I went that way this morning," she said — everyone knew how her cat accompanied her on her early praise-walks — "and I was appalled by all the junk along both sides of the road. Uncle Miltie says no one has taken over the responsibility for picking up along that stretch since Harry Judson took ill last winter."

Barb Jennings, Eternal Hope's choir director and organist, now commented that she believed Harry still hadn't improved much. It was Amy Cantrell, their high school soprano, who suggested, "How about our doing it a time or two — you know, unless Mr. Judson's church or some other group decides to take over?"

Estelle Livett, their indomitable diva, sniffed. "Around here, if you offer to do something 'a time or two,' you're stuck with it forever."

"Well," Amy replied gently, "it does seem like a worthwhile project — and it would be best to do it now, before the stuff's covered with leaves, then snow."

She realized that Estelle was about to argue, and quickly added, "I'd be willing to help one of these Saturday mornings if Abe can give me time off from the deli — or if we can start really early on another day."

Enthusiasm for the clean-up project wasn't unanimous. Some choir members were frankly uninterested. But enough of them agreed to meet there Saturday morning that Amy looked around at her

10

friends and beamed. Les said he'd make sure they had the proper supplies, and Gracie agreed to approach the other church.

"I'll encourage someone in Harry's own congregation to head up a crew more permanently, until he's better," she told them.

Gracie brought the Turner twins, Tish and Tyne, and had expected to be the first to arrive at the agreed-upon end of Ferris Road. But Les was already there and had set up a large sandwich-board caution sign. He greeted them cheerfully as he took a carton from his van, "Good morning, ladies.

"There's everything you'll need here, Gracie," he told her. "Now I'll take the rest of this stuff down the road to the other half of our gang."

"Fine. We might as well get going!" Gracie was grateful that he had organized things so well.

"We'll be working our way back in this direction." He looked at the debris along both sides of the shady road, then back at her. "Everyone needs to wear one of these reflective vests and use plastic gloves, and each of you should be sure to carry an extra trash bag or two."

Tish was already pulling on her gloves, as

was her twin sister. "We'll begin right here. . . ."

And Tyne added, ". . . on the left side of the road."

Gracie never failed to find amusement in their twinnish habits, like finishing each other's sentences. Though they were married, both women expected their husbands to understand just how powerful their own particular brand of sisterhood was.

Now Amy pulled up, accompanied by Mark Canfield, a friend of hers whose mother, Sally, was a former choir member.

Gracie greeted him with affection. She'd taught him for several years of Vacation Bible School, back when he was a towheaded boy given to keeping frogs and little lizards in his backpack. *Where does the time go, Lord? Now he's practically a man and more interested in pretty Amy than in what he might fish out of a stream.*

"So you want the two of us to take that side of the road?" Amy asked, donning her plastic vest.

Mark added, "Sounds good to me. We'll help on whichever side we're most needed." Gracie couldn't help but feel proud of their willingness to help by getting up early and giving up their Saturday morning.

Two other vehicles arrived, and Les

talked to their drivers before returning to his car and calling through the open window as he eased by, "Don's leaving his car here and Barb's dropping off hers near the one-mile mark. They will ride the rest of the way with me, and when we meet halfway, Barb will drive me back for mine. We'll have plenty of room in the two vehicles for all of us to get back here."

Gracie dropped a sticky Styrofoam box and two beer cans into her trash bag as she straightened. "That sounds like an excellent plan." *Thank You, Lord, for making sure that when we, Your humble hearts and hands, start a project we also have a head to organize us.*

After the others left, conversation in Gracie's group first centered on the task at hand and then on the lovely mid-October day. Naturally, however, they were soon off on other subjects. "How's your mother, Mark?" Gracie asked.

"Good — she really likes what she's doing at school."

"She's still a personal aid to that little Macfarland girl?"

"Um-hmmm." He was down in the ditch picking up shards of a broken jar, empty cigarette wrappers, soda cans and soggy newspapers. "But Lynn's not so little anymore. She's ten — and Mom says she's doing a

whole lot better with her school work."

He was energetically rooting amidst over-grown grasses and weeds for more junk. He looked up at Gracie. "Mom spends most of her time with Lynn. It's really her major re-sponsibility."

"I recall how hard she worked to become fluent in sign language."

"Yeah. But she doesn't use that as much now. Lynn's also gotten pretty good at reading lips, and that means she's caught up with her class in most subjects."

Gracie smiled her approval.

"But she hasn't caught up with math," Mark added. "And she doesn't speak a lot — not *yet,* Mom says."

Gracie would never forget the child's bout with meningitis when she was only two years old. Up until then, little Lynn Macfarland had been a happy, chattering youngster with a bright and bubbly person-ality.

Everyone loved Lynn, Gracie recalled. *There must have been hundreds — thousands! — of prayers going up to You, God, from all of us while she was so sick. There were times at the beginning when she didn't seem to respond at all, when we feared she'd remain little more than a vegetable, and it seemed You maybe weren't listening or caring.*

14

Thank You, Father, for Sally's steady assistance and for the Macfarland family's faith and love — and for Lynn, herself. For her courage and the example she sets. And please help her to make the progress she needs in math.

Gracie now picked up a crumpled, dirty, child's coloring book. How did it wind up here? Possibly some boy or girl had thrown it from the window of a passing car? Gracie couldn't resist glancing at the pages but, seeing no name or other identification, she dropped it into her bag along with her other "finds."

She enjoyed listening to Amy and Mark talk about their high school and community activities as they worked. The gloves Les had so thoughtfully provided were much appreciated when they came upon a partially eaten, decayed groundhog!

Mark had just rolled a car tire up the bank when Gracie suggested, "Let's combine all the junk we've collected so far. If we set it by the roadside with the tire, whoever comes with the truck this afternoon can get it."

They passed a large farmhouse as they strolled out Ferris Road, and then three new ranch-style houses. Gracie exchanged greetings with a woman who was working in her garden and a man repairing a fence, and received in turn their appreciation for

15

helping to beautify the area.

A stretch with tall corn growing along both sides of the road seemed especially long to the group as they kept at their surveillance, moving slowly. Tish started to pick up a weathered cardboard box filled with beer cans which, not surprisingly, fell apart. "It can't really be that much harder to dispose of these properly."

"One wouldn't think so," Gracie agreed.

Then Tyne suggested, "Well, I think the law says an underage drinker better not be found with any alcohol in his vehicle."

"That's the big reason so many empties are dumped like this," Mark agreed. He had stepped back from the edge of the road to gather the remains of a forgotten picnic from a field.

Gracie now saw the other half of their group in the distance. Hooray! Mission nearly completed! She offered her help to Amy and Mark, who were gathering scattered nails and a heap of miniature plastic blocks.

"What a mess!" Amy was indignant. "People coming here must just open their doors and throw stuff out!"

Gracie had many times noticed and been annoyed by the paper, boxes, glass, metal and other junk left out in plain sight in

God's gorgeous countryside. The incivility of tossing anything and everything out of car windows and not caring how it looked to others seemed just another indicator of the rise of bad manners when folks should know better.

They'd hardly begun picking up a tangled mass of muddy rags when a car slowed and came to a stop. She felt a moment of guilty pleasure when she heard a familiar voice request, "Hey, everyone, wait a couple minutes before picking up anything else."

Rocco Gravino, editor-in-chief of the *Mason County Gazette*, was climbing out of his small black car with his camera. "I thought I would have been able to get here earlier — but what we've got now looks like it'll work just right for before-and-after shots, to let readers know what a great job you did."

Tish fluffed her blond hair a bit with her fingertips, and Tyne did the same. Mark and Amy reached out at the same time to knock a leaf from Gracie's bright red hair, then both laughed. She thanked them for their attention and for helping her remain respectably tidy for Rocky's readers — but, inwardly, she was wishing for a mirror and a lipstick. Undoubtedly, she told herself, I'd look better covered with leaves and therefore anonymous!

"Abe told me you were out here with some other choir members," Rocky was saying to Amy. "He says you almost never ask for time off, and he felt if you were willing to get out here and muck around, the least he could do was cover for you there."

"Was it awfully busy?"

"Sure, it's a Saturday morning, isn't it?" He dropped a stray bottle into her trash bag. "But no one griped, even jokingly, about the missing waitress. Everyone he told respects you for doing this."

Gracie listened as Rocky teased Amy about her Saturday morning regular customers. But she teased him right back, telling him how she could always tell what he was going to order by looking to see which of his eyebrows was cocked when he walked in the door.

Rocky had just taken his last shots of several completely stuffed black bags, with the Turner twins bookending them when Mark moved beyond where they'd been working and picked up another can.

Gracie saw him do a doubletake and reach back down among the grass and weeds to pick up something. "Wow!" he exclaimed, holding it out on the palm of his hand. "Look at this!"

Amy, glancing over, seemed puzzled by his astonishment. "Okay, I see it, but what is it?"

He looked from her back to the coin, then toward Gracie. "Well, it's not one of those gold-colored dollars — those Sacagawea ones that came out some time ago. That I can see."

He rubbed it against his jeans, trying to clean it. Gracie now walked over to examine it. "It most certainly isn't! Look here, on the back, it says twenty dollars! You know, I suspect it's the real thing, from back in the days when coins were what everyone used instead of paper money."

Amy examined the find. "You're *right*. It says 1930. And it has sort of a squiggle — an *s* — on it."

A large grin appeared on Mark's face as his fingers closed around the coin. "I hope this will be one of those times when the finders-keepers rule prevails."

He looked earnestly at Gracie, and she smiled back encouragingly. "Maybe so. And your doing community service when you found it should be an additional point in your favor!"

Everyone was talking at once, and now it was Rocky's turn to examine the gold coin. He called it a "double eagle." Mark turned it back and forth before pointing out, "There's only one eagle on this, not a double one."

The older man explained, "The ten-dollar coin already had an eagle on it, and was dubbed an eagle. Since the twenty was twice as valuable, people started calling it a 'double eagle.' "

"Oh! That's neat!" Mark continued to turn it around in his fingers.

Tyne handed him a clean handkerchief as he started to put his find in his pocket. "Wrap it in this, just in . . ."

Her sister chimed in, ". . . in case you might have a hole in your pocket, or something."

Gracie laughed. "Then if someone else found it, would it be a doubled double eagle?"

Amy joked, "I think Uncle Miltie is finally starting to wear off on you." She was referring to Gracie's elderly uncle, who lived with her and was famous for his love of corny jokes.

Gracie noticed suddenly that Rocky had moved off and was using his cell phone, but she decided not to call attention to his actions.

Mark now reminded them, "As interesting as this is, we'd better get back to work. We just have a little ways to go."

"Guess what!" Amy shouted, as Les and the others approached. "Mark's found a valuable old gold coin!"

"If I'm not mistaken, this is an especially good date, and in excellent condition." Lester whistled as he peered at the gold surface.

"Do you have any idea what it could be worth?" asked Gracie.

He shook his head. "My dad has a pretty decent coin collection, subscribes to all the magazines and buys the yearly price guides. But, myself, I can't say as how I know much about it, except that a nickel's worth more than a penny."

Barb asked, "But you just indicated you thought this coin might have real value."

"It's only my hunch, based on years of listening to my father and his numismatic pals." He hesitated before adding, "Remember, anything I'd suggest right now would be guesswork."

Gracie saw Mark's eyes brighten. He reached for the wrapped coin in his pocket, touching the outside of it with his palm, making sure it was still there. "Well, any amount would sure help my college fund!"

Gracie nodded. "We all hope we're not raising your hopes." *Dear Lord, remember how impressed Elmo was by this boy, back when he was in Cub Scouts. And Little League. Mark was a fine youngster then and he's a splendid young man now.*

Rocky caught her eye and motioned with a tilt of his head for her to join him a few steps from the others. "I just called the newsroom and asked Sue to check on the value of a 1930-S double eagle."

"And . . . ?"

Both his bushy eyebrows rose, and he grinned. "If it's actually in as good condition as it appears to be — and only a dealer will be able to judge — Mark probably has stumbled upon a coin worth upwards of thirteen thousand dollars, maybe even a bit more."

She stared at her friend. *"Thousand?"*

He repeated the single word. "Thousand."

She turned to look at Mark, who was back at work picking up trash with the others. He and Amy seemed to be in a race to see how many aluminum cans they could lob into an open bag.

When their temporarily adopted stretch of Ferris Road was pronounced immaculate, everyone rode back to the church. There, Tish and Tyne tried at the same time to tell Pastor Paul Meyer the amazing news concerning Mark's double eagle. Then Mark held out the coin for him to see. —

"Wow." Paul told him, turning it over several times, staring at the details of the raised printing on it.

Les joked, "Now we truly believe, Paul, in keeping our eyes cast down in humility, especially when there are rare coins on the ground!"

There was a bit more joking before Mark said, "I've got to go. I've got a number of lawns to mow and need to get one or two taken care of before midday."

He was almost to the edge of the parking lot before Paul hurried after him. Gracie overheard Paul offer to keep the coin in the church's safe until the bank would open on Monday. Good idea, she thought.

Gracie drove Fannie Mae, her aged and faithful blue Cadillac back to the house, eager to tell Uncle Miltie about the coin. However, the note lying on the kitchen table informed her he had headed off to the senior center.

She hardly thought of lunch until, after taking a shower, hunger suddenly reminded her she'd had a long morning and little food. Yes, there was quite a bit of the lamb roast left from the day before, as well as smaller quantities of peas and limas. Cold sliced lamb sandwiches were just the ticket! There was a jar of Joe Searfoss's home-grated horseradish and a loaf of multigrain bread she'd defrosted the day before.

She was just tossing the left-over vegetables in a mayonnaise dressing and adding cherry tomatoes for color when Uncle Miltie walked in the door, leaning lightly on his canes.

"I feel pretty spry today, my girl," he told her, smacking his lips. "If those are lamb sandwiches, I can eat three . . . at least!"

He went to wash his hands at the kitchen sink, but grinned at her over his shoulder. "That's one of the many pleasurable things about your meals, Gracie. One good one always leads to a better one."

She blushed, even though she knew he was right. She was a legendary cook and caterer in Willow Bend but never tired of her own imaginative menus or of her uncle's praise of them.

"I wish I could have helped this morning," he told her.

"Maybe next time. . . ." But she doubted that, even as she answered him. His osteoarthritis was unpredictable, and though he'd gotten back to using his quad canes instead of his walker, leaning to pick up trash over a couple of miles of country road could hardly be considered medically indicated.

But she didn't say that. She diverted him with news of the coin that Mark had discovered. "At least we have the date," she finished. "It's almost as clear as if it was freshly minted."

"Sounds good." He dried his hands and started across the kitchen toward the phone. "While you put my sandwiches on a plate with some chips and salad," he said, winking, "I'll make a quick call to Bernie Jenson. He claims he's not a real collector, but he is. Anyone who can blithely spend a bundle on a single coin, like he's liable to, has got to be pretty serious about it."

Gracie liked getting to Sunday school and church on time — a practice that Uncle Miltie dubbed "bird early" — which was why they hadn't seen the feature story on the choir's trash pickup until they arrived.

Estelle had brought in the second section of the Sunday *Gazette*, just in case the picture of her with the very large bag might go unremarked.

"You can tell who was working hardest," she declared proudly.

This brought a hoot of derision as Les insisted that the bulging bag to her right was the one he'd just tied off, having filled it himself.

"Children, children!" Gracie mock-scolded. "Everyone worked so well out on the job, let's not mess it up now."

They laughed, and Les reminded them,

"It was really fun, though, wasn't it?"

"Yes, it was," Estelle admitted. "More than I expected. To be honest, I had to talk myself into going, but I'm glad I did." She looked as if she had even surprised herself.

Amy had already seen the newspaper article before leaving home. "I wonder why there's no picture of Mark and his double eagle."

"Maybe Rocky didn't take one," Barb said. "I didn't see him do it."

Gracie shook her head. "I'm sure he didn't — probably deliberately."

"Why wouldn't he?" Amy asked her.

Gracie shook her head. "I'm not sure. It certainly would have made the tale of our good deed a lot more colorful!"

It was the church's custom to invite congregants to share their harvest bounty. Looking out over the baskets of produce and flowers from the gardens of Eternal Hope's members, Gracie thought their morning anthem, "The Fruit of the Land Declares God's Glory," to be especially appropriate. The profusion of tomatoes, peppers, squash, eggplants, and melons, as well as the asters and mums, was indeed glorious.

From her vantage point in the choir loft, Gracie hadn't at first noticed Mark seated below with his mother. Sally Canfield was a regular attendee and had once sung in the choir. But her son had stopped coming when he was about fifteen. Gracie understood the irregular habits of teenagers, even when it came to something as important as worship.

And now, today, Mark Canfield was here! *I wonder if Amy's bringing him yesterday has something to do with his turning up today, Lord. I hope it's not just because of his finding that double eagle.* But then she reconsidered. *No, that's not right. If that should turn out to be his reason, then it's because You have chosen his path of return. The coin is just that — a mere coin — while Yours is the gold that never dims or tarnishes.*

Heading home, Gracie decided to detour by Ferris Road. The massed trashbags were still awaiting pickup, as she'd hoped. She wanted Uncle Miltie to see what the choir had accomplished.

"Gosh!" he told her, "And golly! It's what I call a *haul* lot of junk!"

"Pretty funny!" Gracie retorted. "Les has arranged for someone to come and cart it away tomorrow morning, I believe. And I'm still feeling it in some muscles!"

"Was the coin found right out in the open?" Uncle Miltie now was curious.

"Not really. With the weeds and grass as tall as they are, if Mark hadn't been looking for something to pick up, he might not have seen it."

On the way back to town, her uncle suggested stopping at Abe's Deli.

"You may be Willow Bend's best cook," he said, chuckling, "dedicated to feeding me and one very large cat, along with all your catering clients . . . but a cheese danish or a poppyseed bagel just aren't in your repertoire!"

"My friends." Abe Wasserman's face was one big smile as he came around from behind the counter to hug Gracie. "The service must have been longer than usual."

"It was the route from the church to here that was longer," Uncle Miltie told him. "Gracie took me out to see where they were uncovering treasure yesterday along Ferris Road."

"I heard from Amy about the coin Mark found — and then there was that great spread in this morning's paper! Some people sure have pull!"

Her uncle was smug. "It's her lemon cake, or maybe her chili! No, seriously, our Rocky is simply a good editor, you know, with that finely tuned sense of what people like to read."

"You're right about that! Everybody who's come in today has been talking about it." He chuckled. "Of course a couple of Harry Judson's fellow Presbyterians were annoyed about their never having been written up during all their years of doing the policing out there — and now you folks getting it the very first time!"

Returning with the blintzes and applesauce Gracie had ordered and Uncle Miltie's scrambled eggs with toasted bagel, Abe looked at them quizzically.

"Know anything about that gold coin that was found?" he asked while pouring coffee.

"Only that it's a double eagle." She was sure he was savvy enough to understand its possible value.

"Amy seems to like Mark a good deal. I know her well — and the fact that she asked him to accompany her is indicative of her feeling for him, I'm certain," said Abe.

"Are they seeing a lot of each other?" Uncle Miltie wanted to know. "Going out together?"

"Well," said Abe slowly. "I'm not keeping tabs on what she does when she's not helping out here, but Mark has waited for her often over the past few weeks."

"I understand he's trying to save money for school," Gracie put in.

"Could be." Abe moved away to refill the cups of several other patrons and to chat before returning. He continued, "And Mark's a good worker, you know. He's mowed my yard for me at the house these last two years, and is meticulous about trimming around bushes and walks."

"That's good to know."

"I'd give a positive recommendation to anyone who might be considering hiring him."

"Huh!" Uncle Miltie snorted, seeing their neighbor emerge from her house just as Gracie was pulling to a stop. "She's been watching for you."

Gracie smiled at him, opened her door and got out, calling, "What's up?"

Marge Lawrence looked conspiratorial as she joined them. "How close were you to Mark when he found that coin?" She winked.

"How *close* were we?" Gracie repeated, wondering what that had to do with anything. However, with her best friend appearing so serious, she answered, "Well, he'd been down in a ditch — well, not a ditch, actually, more like a shallow trough or something — where the run-off from the road goes. There's a lot of grass and weeds there, so he was checking all that out while taking a step or two back onto the road."

"Was the coin on the road itself?"

"We-e-ell, Ferris Road's one of those where each year or so they put down another layer of gravel and tar or bitumen or whatever, but there's space along the side that's loose pebbles and stuff. . . ."

"Yes," Uncle Miltie put in. "A lot of our less-traveled roads are like that. We used to call 'em 'tar-and-chip roads.' "

"So that's where he supposedly found the coin?"

"Supposedly? What's going on? I think it was more where there's grass or weeds growing, just beyond the hard surface."

"Then you didn't actually see him find it? You didn't see him pick it up off the ground?"

"I don't like the direction these questions are going," Gracie frowned. "You were out there, too, yesterday morning. Did you actually watch where each person was as he picked up each can or paper?"

"Of course not — but I hoped you had this one time."

"Okay, spill it." Uncle Miltie was annoyed at her taking so long to get to the point. "If we have to deal with some problem, we need to know what it's about."

Marge's lips pursed. "Pastor Paul asked me to have you call as soon as you got back."

Gracie wondered what their minister wanted, and she wished Marge wouldn't make them drag what she had to say out of her, sentence by sentence.

They were inside the house by the time she got it all out. "Miles Stevens — you know him, of course, since he worked at the First National Bank just about forever. Well, he's heard about Mark's finding the coin, and now claims it's *his*, that Mark stole it from him."

"That's absurd!" Gracie came to a full stop and stood there staring at her friend. "He was with us, and Miles wasn't. And that boy did find the coin out there."

"I never did trust that man," Uncle Miltie declared, "even if he did work in a bank."

First National's board of directors obviously had considered Mr. Miles Stevens trustworthy. Gracie herself, however, had sometimes felt he was a little sneaky-seeming. "There's got to be something going on here that we're not aware of — that we don't understand." She looked at Marge. "How did you hear about this, Marge?"

"It was Pastor Paul. I saw him stop here a

while ago, so I came out and asked if there was anything I could do — if I might give you a message when you got back."

"We went out to Ferris Road, then stopped at Abe's for lunch," said Gracie. "I'd wanted to show Uncle Miltie where we were working and how much we'd picked up."

Gracie knew the parsonage number almost as well as her own, so it was only a few seconds before she heard, "Pastor Meyer speaking. Can I help you?"

"Paul, this is Gracie. Marge just gave me a strange story about Miles Stevens claiming that Mark's coin is *his*."

"That's what he's saying."

"That's ridiculous!" But then she remembered hearing Paul's offer to put the coin in the church's safe. "He hasn't seen it, has he? You didn't show it to him?"

"Of course not! But he's heard that Mark has a 1930-S double eagle, and he claims he had one, which is now missing. And that since the choir sponsored the clean-up, *I'm* responsible."

"And just how would that coin get from Miles Stevens's possession to the weeds along Ferris Road?" Gracie demanded. "Was he strolling along out there and dropped it? It's unChristian of me to doubt

34

him, I know, but it seems, shall we say, highly unlikely."

"I guess . . ."

"For that matter," she went on, unintentionally interrupting, "I've never seen Miles out walking at all. And as you know, I do a lot of that."

"That's true."

"This whole thing sounds fishy to me!" Gracie's eyes flashed. Uncle Miltie pretended to cower, while Marge gave her a thumbs-up.

"What he's saying is that he'd brought a few coins home from his safety deposit box last week. He says they were on the kitchen table last Saturday — a week ago, that is — and Mark was mowing his lawn at that time.

"For some reason or other — oh, yes, Mark came into the house to tell him he needed more gas. Miles says he was 'careless enough' to leave those coins right out there in plain sight while going into the other room to get some money. "So he came back out, gave Mark the money and told him to go over to the Gas-'n'-Go and get the gas can filled."

Gracie now understood. "He claims Mark Canfield just walked out of his house with that particular coin in his pocket?"

"That's what he says. That Mark must

have done exactly that."

"And Miles didn't happen to miss this exceedingly valuable coin," she paused for effect, "for a whole week. Until he heard that Mark had found a 1930-S double eagle!"

"Right you are, dear Gracie. But, like you, I wish it weren't the case."

"Does he know that you actually have the coin in your possession?"

"I didn't think it wise to tell him, not just now. He's already insisting that I get it from Mark and give it to him. Or else be accused of obstructing justice."

"How awful!" she exclaimed. "He can't be serious!"

"Gracie, listen to me. You know I wouldn't do what he was asking, not without talking to Mark and to Herb."

"Do you believe there's a chance Mark might have taken it?" She hated even asking the question.

"No, I don't." A second or two passed before he added, "Let's face it, though, I don't know either of them very well."

Her mind was racing. She suddenly realized that she was trusting Mark completely, believing his version of events, not just because of her own longtime fondness for him but also because of her late husband's judgment regarding the boy's character. Elmo Parks had rarely made any mistakes when it came to assessing a person's moral fiber.

"So Miles thinks Mark just pretended to find the coin along the roadside? That his coming along with Amy to help us was just to give him a useful cover situation?"

"That's his thesis."

An unhappy sigh completely emptied her lungs, and she stood there trying to decide what was best. "So you'll talk to Herb about this? Maybe even before Miles Stevens gets a chance to?"

"Do you know if he's on duty today? I hate to bother our chief of police on his day off."

"I think he was off last weekend. Wasn't he in church? I didn't see him, this morning." She decided to take the plunge and offer to talk to Herb herself. "If you'd like, I could call him."

"Thanks, Gracie." Paul seemed relieved. "I'd be glad to discuss it with him, should he want that. But of course I wasn't there with you yesterday."

Herb Bower was in his office and told her to come over right away if that was convenient. Gracie felt it best to go alone, even though both Uncle Miltie and Marge offered to join her. Admonishing them both not to tell anyone where she was headed or about Miles Stevens's claiming the coin, she strode out resolutely to Fannie Mae, determined to convince Herb Bower that Miles Stevens was accusing Mark unjustly.

Herb met her at the door. "Let's sit here, since nobody's around on this beautiful Sunday afternoon," he suggested, turning around one of the comfortable waiting-room chairs so that they could face one another.

She took her seat, and began straight away. "You know about our cleaning up the Ferris Road trash yesterday?"

"Of course." He grinned as he added, "When you rate the entire front page of the *Gazette*'s second section, that's pretty hard to miss."

She made a wry face. "Rocky was going around taking pictures, but we had no idea he planned to do *that*. However, it's because of what happened yesterday that I'm here right now."

She'd known from previous times when they'd worked things out together that he was an excellent listener. And on this occasion he proved to be so again. He sat there apparently relaxed, leaning back in his chair, ankle crossed over his knee. Even when she finished, his manner appeared casual.

"Do you think it at all unusual that Mark decided to go along with Amy's invitation to help pick up the trash?" he finally asked. "Are they especially good friends?"

Could he be thinking Miles's story was true? But she cautioned herself against jumping to conclusions. "Amy said he came into the deli while she was working after school the other day. She'd just been talking to Abe about coming in late on Saturday, so she turned and asked Mark if he'd ever participated in any cleanups, and he said the only time he'd done so was back when in Cub Scouts, when El had gotten all of them involved."

Herb's eyes and face softened, as did his voice. "That husband of yours touched the lives of so many people in ways we're still realizing."

Unbidden tears threatened to fill Gracie's eyes. El's death had robbed her of her best and most loving friend, the man she respected above all others. She and Herb rested there in sad silence for a moment. Then Gracie sat up straighter and looked him in the eye.

"El thought Mark was a very promising youngster."

"I gather he's an ambitious young man with a lawn-care sideline."

She nodded. "I understand he's got a lot of contented customers — like Abe Wasserman, for instance. He has his mind set on going to college, you see, and he's smart enough to realize his mother's not in any position to give much financial help."

"He's a good student?"

"Good enough. And, as I say, strongly motivated."

But this wasn't dealing with their problem, at least not directly. She drew in a deep breath and asked, "So what should we be doing about that coin?"

Herb regarded her somberly. " 'So what are *we* going to do?' You're beginning to sound like a hardened operator, Gracie, thinking that a little carefully applied muscle can carve out a straight path to the correct resolution. Believe it or not, my friend, sometimes things do work themselves out without our involvement."

"Herb," she assured him, "I accept your line of reasoning. I just wanted to weigh in — not meddle. I promise you."

He stood up, extending his hand to help her to her feet. "I'm glad you did. Had Miles arrived here first with his story, I'd have had to check it out. Now, if and when he does, I'll have more reason to be cautious in questioning him."

"I appreciate that — and you."

She appreciated him even more as he walked her to the door saying, "I do thank you for coming, Gracie — and for your caring so much about the welfare of Willow Bend. It's folks like you who make people like me want to never leave this little corner of Indiana."

She turned and gave him her most engaging smile. "I hope you and Marybeth never do leave, Herb — at least not as long as I'm around."

3

Marge and Uncle Miltie were in the middle of a fast-paced game of double solitaire, so Gracie didn't interrupt, although her fingers did slide lightly across her uncle's shoulders. He could sometimes sound curmudgeonly, but she knew all too well that his crustiness was just the container for a very soft cream filling.

Undoubtedly he had realized that Marge wouldn't leave until Gracie got back and so, to distract her, had suggested the one game that Marge was able to win much of the time. She could drive him mad with her fidgety ways, but he knew how to handle her when he felt like it. Now, when she played her last card, a red queen on a black jack, she crowed, "I beat you again. I've got two games to your one!"

"*Aw*, I wasn't really trying. You know

what a gentleman I am," said Uncle Miltie. And then with a pretend leer, "Always wanting to give the guest — especially such a pretty woman — the chance to win."

"*Ho!* That'll be the day." She made a face at him, but she was pleased.

"So how did you make out, Gracie?"

The reply came from the living room doorway, "I could only give him what little information we have so far to work with. Now we have to see if Miles comes to him with that story."

"I hope he was horrified!"

"Herb Bower wasn't born yesterday," Uncle Miltie stated firmly. "He'll know what to do . . . or not do."

Gracie hurried upstairs. *Well, I think my uncle's right. Herb will have You behind him if Miles goes to him with that story. And of course if there's something You want me to do, please give me the wisdom to recognize what it is.*

She caught a glimpse of herself in the mirror and was almost surprised to see a slight smile on her face. *Thanks, Lord, for recharging my spirit each and every time we talk.*

By the time she returned to the kitchen, the pair already there were nearing the end of the current game. "The very last one," her uncle declared firmly. "I can't stand to lose any more."

"You're such a poor sport!" Marge teased.

"Sticks and stones," he replied, then glanced toward Gracie. "She promised to play Scrabble with me if I'd sit through one more game of this stupid double solitaire."

"I was just trying to give him another chance to even our score — but, of course, he's not winning."

She dramatically laid the final card on the pile where he'd just placed one of the several he still held. "Can I help it if he's so slow?"

He ignored her and said loudly, "As you can see, my dear Gracie, she's not smart enough to realize I'm letting her win this quickly so she won't back out of her agreement. Scrabble's a serious game."

"You two!" Gracie laughed.

"You know you'd miss it if we were boringly agreeable all the time, with none of this spice and seasoning! It'd be like a bland meal!"

Marge made no effort to hide her laughter as she got up and went to the counter for the Scrabble box. He was methodically separating the playing cards by color, and as she

started to get the other game ready —
turning the lettered wooden squares face-
down upon the table — he was carefully fitting the decks into their proper boxes.

A three-way game ended with Gracie fitting her final *f* below the *i* of the horizontal
word *lit* — thus forming the two-letter ver-
tical word *if.*

"I can't believe it!" Marge cried. "You've
been behind this entire game . . . and now
you've won by one lousy point!"

She glanced at the antique school clock
on the kitchen wall and pushed back from
the table. "Can you believe it's nearly six already? I need to see if I had any calls."

Uncle Miltie also was getting to his feet.
"Sometimes it's better getting messages on
the machine. That way, you don't get
bogged down with long conversations."

"But then *I* have to pay for returning the
long-distance ones."

He headed toward the living room. "Let
them call back. If they don't, you'll know it
either wasn't really important, or they
didn't care enough."

"But that unreturned call might be just
the one that could have turned my social life
around," she said, going out the door.

Marge had spoken lightly, as though

amused by the possibility. But Gracie knew her friend missed having a male friend in her life. As she returned the cards and Scrabble to their cupboard, she sighed.

Seeing the stack of games suddenly reminded her that it had been a whole week since she'd talked with her own son, Arlen, her daughter-in-law Wendy and her wonderful grandson Elmo. It was true she'd been busy, as always — and they were, too — but for the Parks family, that wasn't a good enough excuse.

"Hello, Elmo," she greeted her grandson less than a minute later. "I've been thinking about you and your parents, and just had to call."

"Hi!" His voice was as clear and as real as though he were right here with her in her Willow Bend kitchen. "Mommy! Daddy! Grandma's on the phone!"

She waited, then heard him say, "I've been thinking about you too, Grandma. We went to the zoo today."

"Still like the monkey house best of all?"

"Well, the snakes, they're pretty cool."

As much as she treasured her relationship with her grandson, she couldn't work up much enthusiasm for snakes! "How about the elephants? You thought they were special, too."

"I still do — but then, *every*thing's special, and I know 'cause you told me that."

And then Arlen was on the phone with, "So how's the center of the universe, I mean Willow Bend, Mom?"

"Perfectly beautiful, right now!"

"And you and Gooseberry have been watching the season change during your morning walks," he prompted.

"Yes, we have. Then yesterday morning some of us in the choir went out to gather bags and *bags* of trash from along Ferris Road."

"I didn't realize your choir was adopting that stretch of road. Whose idea was that?"

"Well, in a way mine. And we haven't, really. But the church that had been doing this hasn't taken care of it since early spring. Since I'd noticed how awful the area looked, we wound up organizing to take care of it this one time."

"At least that's something that shouldn't get you in trouble. You're not involved in any major legal or other messes as of now, are you?"

"Of course not. And just because I've been involved in one way or another with a few mysterious happenings doesn't mean I'm trouble-prone, I'll have you know."

Arlen chuckled. "It's important to those

47

of us who love you to make sure that that's the case."

Gracie had anticipated telling him about finding the coin and about Miles Stevens trying to claim it, but now decided to give only the first half of that information.

"Have you any idea how much the coin's worth?" he asked. "Since 1930 seems rather late in the production of gold coins, I'd guess this one's probably not going to wind up valued at more than several hundred dollars."

"There's been no opportunity to have it professionally appraised," she admitted, "but one of Uncle Miltie's friends checked values in the *Blue Book* or *Red Book* or *Green Book* — whatever it is that comes out each year to give current market prices. He says if the coin's determined to be in as good condition as we think it is, it could be worth as much as nineteen thousand dollars!"

"*Oops!* I mean thirteen!"

She smiled as his laughter at having so badly missing the mark came across the wires and into her cozy kitchen.

A moment later, he suggested, "Be sure to persuade Mark to find a secure place for that coin, Mom. Should it be lost or stolen, it'd be almost impossible to prove ownership."

"That's why Paul already has it in the church safe."

"Does anyone else know that?"

"I have no idea."

They were both aware that Willow Bend was a place where everyone was interested in what was going on in the lives of others, though usually not for the wrong reasons. *And let's face it, Lord, I recall a number of times when I've been very grateful for the concern and generosity of these people.*

Gracie now described the sudden appearance of Gooseberry, twining his orange body around her ankles. She looked down and grabbed his tail for an impromptu massage. Gooseberry loved getting a good tail rub.

Arlen chuckled. "I hope nobody ever tells that pet of yours that he's a cat, not a dog. You'd have a thoroughly traumatized feline were he to learn how abnormal he is."

"*Abnormal?* How can you possibly think such a thing?" She bent down and lifted the topic of their conversation one-handedly onto her lap, not the easiest thing to do since he was so large and so entirely relaxed that it was like picking up an inadequately stuffed rag toy. "He's just so much superior to the average cat that poor humans like us haven't got him figured out yet."

"Heaven help us if and when we do!"

His affectionate laughter was joined by hers.

Gracie awoke to the sound of pounding rain and, rolling over, pulled the covers up over her head. No, she didn't expect to go back to sleep, but at the same time had little urge to bound outside for her prayer-walk on a morning like this.

And I don't have a single thing that absolutely has to be done this morning, she crowed. That seemed so unusual that she forced herself to do a mental rundown and realized that, first of all, she needed to write a note on the birthday card she'd bought for 101-year-old Amanda Bixler.

She'd had every intention of doing that on Saturday, but with the trash duty, she hadn't got around to it. She also had intended to whip up an angel food cake, which she and Uncle Miltie could take over to Pleasant Haven this afternoon. With this in mind, she pushed back the covers, got out of bed, and began her day with a hot shower.

Gracie didn't consider pride to be one of her major faults. It was just that she got such satisfaction from using her own recipes, creating desserts and confections from scratch

— most of the time, that was. However, there now was one exception to this self-imposed rule, thanks to a visit to New York City.

When at Arlen's the year before, she'd congratulated Wendy on her delicious, perfect angel food cake — and her daughter-in-law had shown her the boxed mix she had used. So when Gracie returned to Willow Bend a few days later, the bottom of her suitcase was weighted with a number of these boxes. She had two left — soon to be only one after she made Amanda's.

Had anyone asked, she'd have shared her "secret." But, as it was, she just smiled and said, "Thank you," when later she received raves from the elderly ladies at Amanda's end of the hall who were enjoying slices of cake with sliced strawberries and a scoop of ice cream.

After they had visited for over an hour, Gracie dropped her uncle off at the senior center and detoured around by way of the police station. Lucille Murphy, the daytime police dispatcher, greeted her in friendly fashion. "As far as I know, he can see you right away, Gracie, but let me call back there."

It was only a second or so later that Herb came down the short hallway to give a hearty welcome, "Good to see you, Gracie! Come on back to my office."

"I was over at Pleasant Haven to take a birthday cake to Amanda Bixler, and thought I'd stop in here for a few minutes."

She smiled at Lucille, who asked how old Amanda was. "One hundred and one — but doesn't look or act a day over ninety!"

Lucille laughed. "And there aren't many about whom you can say *that*."

Gracie cocked her head thoughtfully. "To me, it's amazing to find as many as there are. Centenarians were extremely rare back when I was a kid." A mere fifty or so years ago, she thought.

As she started down the hallway, she heard the other woman's reply. "When I was a child, I considered everyone over thirty or forty to be an antique — and probably hadn't a clue how much unmapped territory lay between that and being a centenarian!"

"You certainly will never be old, Gracie, not to any of us who know you." Herb laughed as he pulled a chair around to the side of his desk. "And I suppose the fact of my aging at the same rate should make me more aware of my own mortality. But it doesn't, I'm afraid."

"I pray I'll age as gracefully as dear

Amanda," Gracie said as she took the indicated seat. "She didn't have a particularly easy life as a child or adult, yet is such a sweet and forgiving person. Or maybe I should say accepting."

He looked at her with affection. "Don't worry, Gracie, you're all of those things and much, much more."

"Thanks, Herb." She was touched. He was, she knew, not a demonstrative man. To break the mood and return to a more businesslike atmosphere, she asked quickly about the coin.

"Miles has made an appointment to see me an hour from now, but didn't mention what he wants to discuss."

"I — don't suppose you'd be allowed to tell me much anyway, would you?"

He leaned back in his chair and sat there looking at her. "That depends on what's happening, and also what you need to know. After all, it's not like we've never before been on the same team together."

"We-e-ll . . ." She shifted position. "I probably shouldn't be here right now, but something was said over at the home this afternoon that I figured perhaps should be shared. You know Marjorie Printz, who now lives there, don't you?"

"Of course. Even though she was already

retired from elementary school teaching by the time I came, I soon got to know her. For that matter, everyone seems to."

She nodded agreement. "One of the aides mentioned that article in the paper, and then another visitor said she'd heard something about a valuable coin that had been found, and asked about that. I was as evasive as possible, but the reference to a gold coin got Miss Marjorie to reminiscing.

"She told us her father had saved a whole bunch of these — mostly eagles and double eagles — even when they were supposed to have been turned in back in the thirties, when President Roosevelt got the government to pass that law.

"And then she talked about what a godsend they'd been, since teachers didn't make much money thirty years ago. She said that 'nice man,' Miles Stevens, gave her double their face value when she used them as the down payment on her little house on Third Street, where she took care of her dad after his strokes."

"Hunh!" Herb snorted. "How generous!"

"It was all I could do to keep from blurting out something to that effect." Even talking about it now made her angry. "Marjorie added that the so-helpful bank officer told her to keep this a secret, so her father wouldn't be sent to jail for disobeying that terrible law about melting down all the gold currency.

"So to this day she's still thankful for Miles's being so considerate, for taking on himself the risk involved from owning those coins, and assuring her she need never again worry about the possibility of her father being imprisoned!"

"Some benefactor!"

She nodded. "I got to fretting on my way home that if he still has all of those — if he hasn't already sold them for scads of money, that is — that that might give more credibility to his claim that he's the owner of Mark's coin."

Herb came and sat on the corner of the desk nearest her. "Perhaps. But if that does seem to be happening, I may ask for his entire list of the coins, which I doubt will make him very happy."

"Herb," she began, looking thoughtful, "is it logical that he'd bring home just a few at a time from his safe deposit box, as he's apparently claiming?"

"I suppose that makes as much sense as it does for reclusive art collectors to have guarded, secluded, air conditioned galleries in which to keep their most treasured works. They evidently go in there all by themselves to enjoy looking at — and gloating over — what they own." He looked thoughtful, then glanced at his watch.

Gracie would have enjoyed staying longer, but Herb's time was valuable. And she had been grabbing more than her share over the past couple of days.

The sun was trying to break through the clouds, and the sidewalks had dried off. At home Gooseberry came to meet her at the door. He looked up at her with those innocent wide eyes and gave a slightly pitiful, *"Meow."*

Gracie weakened. "Okay, big guy, you win," she told him, laying her purse on the counter and putting the house key in her pocket. "However," she said, letting him lead the way out of the kitchen door, "to be perfectly honest, I need to get out now and get some exercise every bit as much as you do.

"But don't get your hopes too high, dear friend, for this may be just a break in the clouds. After all, the TV weatherman stated it was probably going to rain off and on all day."

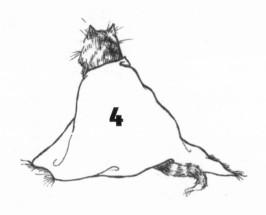

4

She'd told herself Herb would be too busy to bother with reporting to her anything about his interview with Miles Stevens. Yet as she neared home after her walk, she began to walk faster. She opened the door, went inside — and saw no blinking light on her answering machine.

Oh, well, I have no badge, she reminded herself. My capacity is purely unofficial.

Things had looked quiet enough while she was there, but he undoubtedly had mountains of paperwork, as well as myriad phone calls and people coming and going. He could have gotten called out, too, for some reason.

Gracie smiled a little, remembering when he'd first come to Willow Bend as an officer. Back then, he had been even more reserved in his dealing with people. But it made sense. Since he'd been fairly young and there might have been some attempts to take advantage of his inexperience.

There were, of course, always going to be those citizens of Willow Bend whom he'd catch doing things outside the law who wouldn't like him much. But for the most part there was only respect and gratitude. As for Gracie herself, she knew beyond a shadow of a doubt that he was sincerely trying to be the best policeman, and the best Christian he could be.

Thank You, God, for sending Herb here. I know, because Marybeth has confided in me, that he's had opportunities to go to bigger places where he'd earn more money. But Willow Bend is their home, and the people who live here are their brothers and sisters. Do keep him safe, Lord. He has a difficult job and sometimes a dangerous one. Whenever there are ways in which I can be of assistance to him and his family, please help me see what they are.

Uncle Miltie had said he'd get a ride home, and he did — at 3:15. It had slipped her mind that this was a day when he and two others from the senior center were going to the school to read to the littlest kids. But he talked of nothing else while she put dinner out for them.

After offering the prayer of thanks for the

food, he added, "And thanks also for all those youngsters we spent time with this afternoon and for their teachers and the helpers. Some of those kids need so much help, like that deaf girl, Lynn."

Realizing that the child he mentioned was Mark's mother's charge, Gracie asked about her progress.

"You should see Sally's hands and fingers fly as she signs!" he exclaimed. "Even though Lynn's lipreading is improving, Sally signs as a back-up. I was tickled pink we got the chance to stop by her classroom after our reading session. It was only because Sid's daughter, Liz, is her teacher. I asked her how Lynn's getting along, and she told us that this year she's near the top of her class academically."

"That's wonderful."

"Sure is." He finally helped himself to the salmon croquettes and Gracie's special dill sauce. "I didn't get to hear her talk. Liz says she can now, though not everyone can understand her.

"But you know what? Liz and Sally agreed it might be good for Lynn to practice her lipreading with a new person, get used to different speech patterns. I've got the time, so I said I'll go over there at least twice a week, and she and I will work on it during part of her study-period. I start tomorrow. Should be a snap. I'll just tell her jokes."

"George Morgan!" she said sternly. "Be careful! That could set her back! Seriously, though, when will you do it?"

"Sally's going to get back to me. Right now, it'll probably be at 10:05 tomorrow morning. Then I could also do it one afternoon."

It was only later in the evening that Gracie understood how very important this project was to him. Her uncle had been thinking hard about the responsibility he was accepting.

"You know, Gracie, I'm beginning to think I should never have volunteered for that lipreading stuff! It seemed like such a good idea — but I was just looking in the mirror and saying different words. They all look alike! It's not going to be as easy a job as it sounds. If I exaggerate to make each word clear, it won't be natural. How can I be any help, really?"

"It does seem formidable," she agreed, looking up from reading the paper, "but it must be possible, since so many people do it."

He was nearly to his favorite recliner, but stopped and looked at her, then back at the door of the bathroom. Neither of them said anything else, but there was a smile on her face as she realized that he was turning around. Soon she could hear his murmuring, as he practiced in front of the mirror, telling himself jokes.

Going to the police station again the next morning, near the end of her walk, Gracie tried to ignore the label her own mother might have applied to her: "nosey posy." And there were other equally unflattering ways to describe those who took too active an interest in the business of others.

She preferred thinking of it as "being genuinely concerned." But was she only fooling herself?

And wasn't it possible that Herb just might have called when she was out but didn't want to leave a message?

"Wow, twice in two days!" Lucille greeted her. But then, she added, "That must mean things aren't going well in Willow Bend."

It's too close to the truth to be funny, Gracie thought. But she laughed anyway. "It's nothing important. Gooseberry and I were just going by, and I saw Herb's car out back. There is something I'd forgotten to tell him."

Her big orange cat, however, never one to

stand on ceremony, had already strolled the short distance to Herb's office and proceeded inside. She heard Herb's voice greeting, "Well, well, Gooseberry, so you've come to visit me this morning. Shall we go out and welcome Gracie and invite her back here, too?"

Lucille gave a wave of her hand. "Might as well do as the boss suggests."

"I guess so." Laughing, Gracie headed down the hall. "I don't want to bother you if you're real busy, Herb."

"You're not. For that matter, I was just thinking that I should call you and this is much better." He added, "There's not much new, really. Miles Stevens merely wanted to repeat his claim that Mark, and Mark alone, had the opportunity to see the coin and to steal it, since no one else even knew that he had the gold."

"There's Marjorie Printz," Gracie pointed out. "Maybe she's an elderly cat burglar who leaves Pleasant Haven late at night to sneak around reclaiming whatever she thinks is rightfully hers."

He grinned. "As an officer of the law, I'm supposed to keep an open mind concerning opportunity when it comes to the commission of crimes . . . but *that,* my dear Ms. Parks, goes beyond even the limits of my fertile imagination!"

"Well, you can't say I didn't try!" Gracie pretended to puff a pipe à la Sherlock Holmes. "Seriously, though, Herb, if he actually did bring home just a few of his treasured coins, wouldn't he have noticed if one was missing?"

He shrugged. "I asked him that, and he explained that he'd covered all of them with a paper before going into the other room for the money to give to Mark for the gas. And afterward, when the boy had gone outside, Miles just gathered up what had been on the table and put it all into one of those semitransparent glassine envelopes, which he then put in a locked drawer.

"And," he said, noticing her troubled expression, "he didn't check them again until he heard about Mark's finding a gold coin."

"That sounds more plausible than I wish it did," she finally admitted. "But I still don't believe Mark stole anything from anyone!"

It was late that afternoon when Gracie called Sally Canfield at home, on the pretense of discussing her possible rejoining of the choir.

"We've missed you. I'll bet you can't say truthfully you haven't missed us!"

"I loved singing with you, you're right," Sally admitted. "But I've got so very much on my plate right now, Gracie, what with working at school and keeping things under control here at home. I *am* still teaching the young teens class there in the Sunday school."

"I'm truly grateful for that," Gracie reassured her. "If there's ever an age when children need encouragement and tender, loving care, as well as good biblical teaching, it's those early adolescent years."

"My sentiments exactly! And I want to again thank you for your part in making it possible for me to continue teaching them."

Gracie winced inwardly, remembering when there had been some discussion about Sally's removal from her Sunday school class when she was divorced. It wasn't as if she'd been the guilty party, for goodness sake. It had been her husband Arnold who had done the leaving and forced the dissolution of the Canfield marriage.

"You're more than welcome, Sally. I think you're terrific and you know it."

"Yes, I do . . . and I'll confess that I've been holding onto that assurance especially closely the last day or two."

That sounded as though she had a special need, but Gracie wasn't sure just how to respond. Fortunately, Sally went on, "Mark was so excited when he found that gold coin on Saturday! He's such a good boy, Gracie, and such a hard-working student. He's been saving to get a little nest egg together toward going to college. So this at first seemed like a godsend to him — and to me — until Miles Stevens started accusing him of stealing that money from him."

"I'd — heard about that."

"Oh, dear!"

She was obviously distressed, and Gracie hastened to add, "I'm pretty certain nobody believes it."

"I wish I could believe that, Gracie, but I've had personal experience as to how little it takes in Willow Bend to start rumors and keep them going."

That was all too true, unfortunately. "Well, I certainly don't believe it, nor does our chief of police!"

"Herb!"

"Yes, I stopped in to talk to him for a couple of minutes, and he told me Miles had been to see him."

"What about?"

I'm not sure Herb's going to be happy about my telling her this, Gracie thought, but she has to know. "That the double eagle was there on his kitchen table, with other coins, and that Mark must have seen it and taken it when Miles went into the other room to get him the gas money."

Gracie heard a long intake of breath. "That's what he insisted when he came here."

"Miles? He came to your home?"

"He most certainly did! It was awful, really, and he was insisting that Mark give the coin to him right then and there."

"Gosh," Gracie was thinking out loud, "it's a good thing Paul has it in the church's safe. Miles doesn't know that's where it is, does he?"

"I'm sure he doesn't." There was the briefest of pauses before Sally added, "But I wasn't aware until now that anyone knew that except Paul, Mark, and me."

Gracie hastened again to give reassurance. "I happened to overhear Paul make that offer, and was pleased when Mark agreed. Under the circumstances, it's probably the best thing if nobody else learns where it is."

There was the sound of a worried sigh. "You . . . don't think there could be a break-in, do you?"

"Well, Paul's offer was to keep it only until the bank opened on Monday, but I guess Mark has seen no reason to move it. I suspect that the main reason Miles came to your house was his hope of bullying you and your son into handing the coin over right then and there."

"Well, we might have considered it! Let's face it, Gracie! It was awful having him threaten us! And he did! With a lawsuit!"

"Well, until this all gets sorted out, I'm going to be doing a lot of praying!"

"That's wonderful, Gracie. I do thank you for that, and for your friendship."

She was about to hang up when she suddenly remembered something else she'd wanted to mention. "Uncle Miltie's really excited about the possibility of helping with Lynn's lipreading."

"He's such a fine man, so generous with his time."

Her voice had softened with the change of topic, and Gracie went on. "He's concerned as to whether he can actually do it, however. In fact, I heard him practicing in front of the bathroom mirror, trying to make his mouth do whatever's necessary in order for her to 'see' the words."

"I know just how he feels!" Sally chuckled. "My first thought was that it wasn't possible — then that it *might* be possible, just not by me."

"Uncle Miltie says she's very bright."

"She is. I have high hopes for her and her future."

"And I'm sure she senses that, which gives her additional motivation to keep on doing her best for you."

After mulling over the conversation with Sally for a while, Gracie decided to call Herb, in case he wasn't aware that Miles Stevens had actually threatened Sally and Mark. But, missing him at the police station, she left a message that, although it was no emergency, she'd appreciate a call at his convenience.

Taking her at her word, Herb didn't get back to her for over twenty-four hours. Gracie managed with no trouble to stay busy, but her mind kept going to Sally's story of Miles's threat. The next day the phone rang bright and early.

"Good morning, Gracie. I know it's early, but I was afraid I'd miss you, that you'd already be out with Gooseberry for your ramble."

She glanced at the clock. "I had several things I wanted to do first."

"Look, if this is a bad time, you can get back to me later."

"Actually, it's a good time, and I'm glad to hear from you. What I wanted to say probably isn't too important, anyway. But I simply didn't know if you were aware that Miles had gone over to the Canfields' and threatened them with legal action if they didn't hand over *his* gold coin right away."

"They didn't, did they?"

He sounded so concerned that she had to reassure him before asking, "If he should find out that it's in the church's safe, do you suppose he might make trouble for Paul or for our church? Maybe it's the right time to turn it over to the bank. To put it there for safekeeping."

"I suppose so."

She suggested, "Since this coin is the center of so much contention, is it possible — is it ever *done* to have the item held by the chief of police or someone like that? Forget the bank?"

"Really, Gracie . . ."

"I don't mean to ask you to consider doing anything improper."

"Dear Gracie, don't you think I know that, after all this time? I was just about to say that I might have offered to do it myself. I didn't want to take the chance, though, that Sally might think I believe her son to be a thief."

"Oh!" Gracie appreciated Herb's tact.

"What do you feel is best now, at this

stage — for me to make that offer, or you?"

Life sure comes with lots of decisions, Lord! "I can, if you'd like. She already knows we've been in touch, so your offer shouldn't come as a surprise. And I suppose she'll want to talk with Paul, too — she'd have to, I guess, since he's the one keeping the coin now."

The coin transfer was made early the following morning, before Mark and his mother had to leave for school. At the station Herb took the coin from Mark and Paul. Then the police chief carefully sealed it in a marked envelope and placed it in his safe. Closing the heavy door, Herb spun the dial, then requested each observer sign a document as a witness to what he had done.

Gracie realized she wasn't the only one who had been holding her breath.

"There!"

Sally was standing taller, as if a load had been removed from her shoulders. "I appreciate your taking care of it up until now, Paul," she told their pastor, "but I suspect you are glad no longer to have the responsibility for it. I wouldn't blame you."

Paul looked at her gravely. "I didn't lose sleep over its being where it was, but, yes, I'll confess to being relieved it's here."

Choir practice that night went remarkably well. Rick Harding, one of their tenors, who'd been unable to make the cleanup on Saturday, claimed he was ready and able the next time if he could be promised as much excitement as this one had engendered. Not to mention the media attention!

Lester immediately whipped out a pen and piece of paper. "Okay, you can sign up right here, right now. This way, we'll be ready should Harry Judson's fellow congregants not follow through on their commitment to fill in for him."

"If I were *they*," Marge stated dramatically, "I wouldn't let anybody else even have a chance at it! Harry'll probably recuperate faster, too, so he can resume cleanup control of the area, without any help! Who knows what'll turn up next."

"What about that coin Mark found?" Amy seemed concerned. "He does get to keep it, doesn't he?"

"Well," Gracie began. "What happened . . ."

Marge interrupted, "Everyone seems to know that Miles Stevens is insisting it's missing from his collection, that Mark stole it from him and planted it by the roadside."

That rather bald announcement was obviously upsetting to some. Tish immediately came to Mark's defense, "Sally's son is such a nice boy. I can't believe he would ever do anything like that."

"We're quite sure he didn't," Gracie stated flatly. She glared at Marge.

Don Delano spoke up from the baritone section, "I can't believe that of him, either! He's in one of my classes, and I can tell you I've never seen or heard anything about him to indicate he's got an honesty problem. He's a good kid."

Marge added, "I heard Miles has actually already threatened legal action if he doesn't get it back." She was ignoring Gracie's look of entreaty.

Herb's wife, Marybeth Bower, said nothing, and Gracie knew that Herb was far too professional to confide in her any troublesome work issues. She did not interrupt for another minute or two, then deliberately asked Barb something about the anthem they'd be singing on Sunday.

The director looked at Amy. "You'll be here, won't you?"

"Sure. My mother and I were planning to go to Chicago, but that's next weekend."

"Good!"

Barb dreaded changes in any of her plans, especially when it involved solo parts. However, Gracie sensed Estelle's restless movement beside her, and realized the older soprano would never lose her desire to outdo Amy in solo parts whenever possible. But Amy's reassurance to Barb meant that Estelle now was foiled again. Gracie stifled a guilty chuckle.

Amy sang her part beautifully, even on the third page with its tricky change of key and extra-high notes. She had such natural talent and true pitch that Gracie marveled, as she always did, at the girl's ability.

It was after practice that Marybeth took Gracie aside. Herb, it seems, had asked her to tell Gracie that he'd appreciate a call at home. No, she didn't know what it was about, but he'd implied that he'd hoped it could be tonight, if possible.

Gracie thanked her friend and said she'd phone as soon as she got home. Uncle Miltie was glued to the TV, so she had plenty of privacy when she seated herself in the kitchen.

"Marybeth said she gave you my message." It was Herb who'd answered. "I'm glad. It wasn't necessary to talk tonight, but I wanted to make you aware of another new development.

"Have you by any chance heard of a young man called Clark Harrington?"

"I — don't think so, Herb. Should I?"

"Probably not. I hadn't. But this guy came into the station just as I was getting ready to leave — and we now have a third person insisting that the double eagle belongs to him!"

"What!" Gracie could hardly believe her ears.

"It's not a very strong story, but his claim is he inherited it from his grandfather. He says he carries it in his pocket as sort of a good luck piece."

"So, how did it happen to wind up on Ferris Road?"

"His explanation is that it must have dropped out of his pocket when he was out walking in just that spot. What he told me is when he pulled his handkerchief out of his pocket, the coin must have come, too."

"Did he have the location right?"

"Sure, but at this point everyone from here to the Canadian border could pinpoint it on a map!"

She couldn't argue. "When does he say he first missed it? And why would he just walk around with something so valuable?"

"Sunday. But even then he figured it must be around somewhere. Once he heard about Mark's coin, however, he made a careful search for it. As for being heedless with something so valuable, the short answer is, people are like that. That's all."

"Where does he live?"

"He gave an address in Akron, but he's been in Willow Bend for about a week, staying at Cordelia Fountain's tourist home. He's here on business."

"Oh, dear." To her, this sounded more probable than Miles Stevens's claim. Still, doubts lingered. "Can he prove he ever even owned such a coin? Is it insured or anything?"

"He didn't say, but we didn't talk long. I'll undoubtedly be seeing him again soon."

"Oh, dear," Gracie repeated.

5

Gracie didn't enjoy a restful night. She fell asleep fairly quickly, but was wide awake by 1:30 a.m. After that, her mind was racing.

Thank goodness this doesn't happen often, she thought. She kept going over and over the same questions and concerns as she tossed and turned. She felt particularly lonely — something she kept thinking would cease to bother her this way.

I still miss you so very much, Elmo, physically and mentally and even spiritually. You were so much a part of me, and so wise, and so close to God. How I'd love to talk to you — you with your cool head and your warm heart. About this coin business: I'm sure I'm not seeing something important. There seemed little possibility that each of the three claimants honestly believed he was telling the truth, which meant two of them probably were not.

But which two?

She still couldn't believe that Mark ever would have plotted to hide the coin in his pocket, then pretend to find it. It was true that the coin hadn't seemed terribly dirty when she first saw it, but then she distinctly remembered his rubbing it on his jeans. Could he really be such a clever actor . . . and thief?

Miles Stevens she knew she didn't trust, but this new claimant, this Clark Harrington, was an unknown entity.

Gracie considered herself to be, by nature, a person who looked for the best in others. Her dear Elmo, her loving El, used to tease her about it. But, sometimes, even he would be exasperated if she'd persist in "always arguing for the defense."

She was still awake at 3:45. Yet she didn't feel like starting her day that early. Turning on her bedside light, she reached for her Bible and began scanning some of the italicized words at the beginning of chapters.

When nothing caught her attention right away, she went to the concordance and looked for the references under *coin(s)*. There were only a few listed, most in the Gospels. The first Gospel reference concerned someone's bringing Jesus a coin.

The second was about a woman who, having lost and found a coin, invited all of her neighbors to celebrate with her.

The third reference was to Jesus' commendation of the very poor woman who gave to God the last coins she had. The last recounted Jesus' anger at the temple moneychangers who had been stealing from the worshipers. He caused the villains to spill their coins onto the floor before He chased them away.

She pondered these lessons for a time. Although she could certainly understand and appreciate each of them, the only one that felt emotionally right at the moment was the final one.

She decided to pursue her biblical investigations further and check all the references to *money*. Suddenly, she closed the book, remembering the perfect verse without reading it: "The love of money is the root of all evils."

Her hand lightly caressed the soft brown leather as she remembered El's giving this Revised Standard Version to her the first Christmas after they were married. Slowly reopening it, she turned to the sixth chapter of Paul's first letter to Timothy and read, "There is great gain in godliness with contentment; for we brought nothing into the world, and we cannot take anything out of the world; but if we have food and clothing, with these we shall be content.

"But those who desire to be rich fall into temptation, into a snare, into many senseless and hurtful desires that plunge men into ruin and destruction. For the love of money is the root of all evils; it is through this craving that some have wandered away from the faith and pierced their hearts with many pangs."

How true, how very true, dear God, even two thousand years later.

She turned off the light and snuggled down under the covers once again. It was still dark, and she didn't look at the clock to see what time it was. She was content. And she surely felt loved — by God, certainly, but it was also as though El had been there to reveal those words to her.

Morning arrived soon. It was another beautiful autumn day, as shown by the leaves outside her bedroom window. She got out of bed and dressed quickly, eager to be outside with Gooseberry for their walk. Sometimes she listened to music or even, occasionally, to recorded books. Today, however, seemed so special that she wanted just to savor the sights and sounds of nature.

Anxiety over the much-disputed coin

kept trying to intrude, but for the most part she was able to ignore it, if only temporarily. This was a time for enjoying the glorious and grand outpourings of nature's bounty around her.

Then, without realizing it, she found herself walking at the edge of town. Her path had taken her out to Ferris Road. There she saw signs that winter was stalking the brilliant landscape. In the sky, birds were massed and fleeing south.

It was hard to believe that the simple act of trying to restore the roadside to its pristine state had turned out to have such sinister results.

It was too distressing.

She was now strolling along, forcing herself to concentrate on the brilliant yellow of the goldenrod along the sides of the road, and the conical red spikes of sumac. "Both of these are considered unwanted pests or weeds by most people," she mused, "but God most surely must appreciate them, for there are so many growing wild."

A few freshly tossed cans, bottles, and papers were visible, but she tried to ignore them. She was especially disappointed, however, to arrive at that farm lane where they'd spent so much time, and see how messy it had become in less than a week.

Right there was where that controversial coin had been found. Wasn't it strange the way it all had turned out!

Soon Gracie and Gooseberry were back at the main road again, and shortly within the town limits. It would be about the same distance to detour past the police station on her way home as to take her regular route, but she disciplined herself to choose the latter path. "There have been times when I've had to keep in close touch with Herb," she murmured to her four-footed friend who was leading the way, "but I feel there's no need to interrupt his work today."

Back at the house, though, she wasn't so sure. Uncle Miltie greeted her with the message that Sally had already telephoned from school. Twice.

"She sounded perturbed, Gracie, as though she really needed to talk with you."

"Did she leave her number?"

"No — and she said you shouldn't call her there. She'll try to break free for a few minutes later in the morning to try you again."

"Well, I expect to be here." She tried to look and speak calmly. "I was going to take my shower right away, but I'll weed the flower bed by the porch, instead."

"Do you think it's about the coin?" he asked nervously. "What else could it be?"

"I'm afraid it's likely to be the double eagle, but it could be about Joe and Anna's party a week from Sunday. Sally was kind enough to offer to help out in any way she can, even though she really only was related to them by marriage."

He looked more relieved than she felt, and she tried to discipline her thoughts, to take a break from mysterious goings-on and try to think about her plans for that meal.

Anna Searfoss, who was the hostess and who had asked her to cater it, had described it as an "ordinary kind of meal, celebrating our many, many friendships." Anna's nearly sightless eyes had been brimming with happiness as she gave Gracie instructions, knowing how perfectly they would be carried out. They were dear friends and loved to plan parties together.

"Is this your wedding anniversary? Or birthday?" Gracie had asked her friend, certain that those occasions had come and gone already in the year for both Searfosses.

Anna had reached out to lay her hand on her husband's. "Joe and I talked this over a whole lot." She beamed. "We're just doing this as a thank-you, to acknowledge the generosity and loving helpfulness of the people who never fail us."

The couple smiled at Gracie, and Anna

said, "What we most like is your plain, simple, old-fashioned cooking. You know, your special fried chicken, baked beans, scalloped potatoes, cabbage salad, applesauce and . . ."

"Or maybe serve melon chunks instead of the applesauce," Anna said.

Joe put in, "Not those ritzy-ditsy little round balls, but honest-to-goodness chunks. They look more homey that way."

Gracie's glance toward Anna wasn't seen by her, for she had been going blind for years as a result of diabetes. However, her gentle smile and little nod gave agreement.

"And now where were we? Oh yes, we'd like pickled beets and hard-boiled eggs, too. You know, Gracie, Mama grew up in Pennsylvania Dutch country, and she always served pickled beets and eggs for get-togethers."

"I like them, too," Gracie assured her, "and remember how you would bring them to church dinners. However," Gracie paused thoughtfully, "I'll need your recipe for the beets, in order to get the just-right degree of sweet-and-sour."

"We-e-ell, that could be a problem," the elderly woman admitted. "I don't actually have a recipe — I just go by 'guess-and-golly,' as Mama used to say."

Gracie laughed. "A woman after my own heart! My own mother creatively adapted many of the recipes handed down from her grandmother and mother, and I'm delighted to have had them passed on to me. But when my daughter-in-law asks what it means when it says 'add vinegar to taste,' there's no way to explain that without letting her make and taste it!"

"And I'll bet you still don't use a recipe or measure ingredients for making pastry," said Anna, chuckling appreciatively.

The phone rang a few minutes after eleven. Gracie went to answer it with a tremor of apprehension. Better to know than not to know, she told herself. She picked up the receiver.

"Gracie." It was Sally, not even troubling to say hello. "I have only a few minutes. Mark went out and got one of those electronic metal detectors. With money he can ill afford to spend, I might add."

"Why?"

"Well, he's been going back out there to Ferris Road whenever he has even a second's free time. He's making himself ill with worry that Miles will publicly accuse him of stealing that money or even try to take him to court."

Gracie wondered what that had to do with the metal detector. "But . . ."

Sally went on, "He's hoping that if he can possibly find another of those coins, and if only one of Miles's is missing, then that would prove he had nothing to do with it."

"I guess this way he at least feels he's doing something to help himself," Gracie replied sympathetically.

"But he's not sleeping much, and it's hard for him to keep his mind on his studies. In fact, he barely passed an important test yesterday. . . ." Sally sighed heavily. "Maybe you or Herb could talk to him? I'm afraid he's not listening to me."

"I'd gladly do anything I could, but I'm not sure I'd be of much assistance at this point. I've already made it clear to everyone that I saw him find and pick up that double eagle. This business with Miles has come from way, way off in left field, as far as I'm concerned."

She wanted to mention the information Herb had given her last night, about the second claimant, but felt she shouldn't without permission. They talked for another few minutes, and Gracie suspected that when Sally went back to work, her mother-heart would still be as troubled as when she'd picked up the phone to dial Gracie.

Uncle Miltie asked as she went through the living room, "Was that Sally?"

"Yes, dear, it was," Gracie replied. "She's a mother, and I know how mothers feel, especially when circumstances make watchful waiting and its accompanying worry the only course of action."

Uncle Miltie frowned. "Gracie, you'd better get to the bottom of this mess, or I'm going to have to take your private detective's license away!"

"I don't think you're joking — at least not with that glum expression on your face."

"If anyone can make this come out all right, it's you. And pardon me if I'm a stubborn old coot to believe that! But I just *do*."

"I'm proud you have such faith in me," Gracie told him. "But I just haven't got your confidence right now." Shaking her head sadly, she left the room.

"I'm as nervous as a groom!" Uncle Miltie said the next morning. "But I was once a groom, and I don't remember being so agitated!"

"She's just a little girl who's going to be thrilled to have you helping her. Lynn is going to be a wonderful project for you, you'll see."

"But I'm untrained and I'm just going to make things harder for her when I goof up."

Her head was cocked to the side as she challenged, "Did it totally destroy Arlen's self-confidence and verbal development when I couldn't make out his first words as a baby? Or he, mine?"

"Well, no, but . . ."

"And he wasn't even consciously aware of my trying so hard to communicate. Lynn has already come so far, and Sally's been working with her. She's old enough to understand that you have to practice before becoming perfect."

He looked somewhat relieved. Still he fretted, "I'd be satisfied with adequate, forget perfect."

"Then let's leave it to God, okay? You know as well as I do that He's going to be there with you. He's promised that. You'll be doing your best and Lynn's going to be doing her best. That's all it takes, along with the Lord's blessing.

"So today's just your first day. There'll be many more to come, and all along the way you'll see change and improvement. Progress doesn't arrive overnight. It's a process."

As he listened to her, his shoulders straightened. "Thank you, Gracie. So let's get going, right?"

"Yes, Uncle Miltie, let's get going." She followed him out onto the porch. "Right!"

She stopped in front of the school's main entrance, got out his walker and helped him from the front seat. She'd planned to leave the car there while going inside with him, but suddenly two cheerful youngsters of about Lynn's age appeared. "I'm Susan and this is Louise, and we've come to take you to Lynn, Mr. Morgan."

"I'm pleased to meet you, Susan and Louise, and appreciate your doing this. I'd neglected," he told them as he started toward the door, "to learn ahead of time just where I needed to go, and was hoping someone would be around so I could find my way."

Susan ran ahead and held the door wide open, so Gracie suggested, "I'm going to leave since you're in the hands of such capable guides. I'll be home, Uncle Miltie, so just call when you're finished."

Louise looked confused. "I — thought your name was George Morgan."

"You've got it right, Louise," he reassured her. "Uncle Miltie is just a nickname."

Gracie heard the girl ask, "Then — is the lady your niece or not?" Now he'd have to explain how long ago friends had started calling him by the sobriquet given to Milton Berle, a popular old-time entertainer of whom these kids had never heard.

Leaving the school, Gracie found herself once again tempted by the proximity of the police station. But as she drove though the alley, she saw no sign of Herb's car. However, he was coming down the street when she slowed to a stop at the next intersection. Tapping his horn lightly, he beckoned her to follow him back to the police parking area.

"I just dropped Uncle Miltie off and came around this way on my way home. I'm glad I found you."

"And I'm glad I found you," he teased. "Who's the detective around here?" They walked through the back door and down the hall to his office.

Gracie went straight to the point, since it seemed Herb was giving her permission to stay involved with the coin controversy. "Have you found out anything more about our newest claimant?"

"Not much." He shook his head. "Clark Harrington is apparently who he says he is. At least he is working out of Akron,

Ohio — that I found out."

"Anything else?"

His grin was a little crooked. "Well, he's relatively new with his company, but he started there with good references. Even the personnel chief doesn't know much about him, but he's found no reason to do further checking."

"Where was he before?"

"Illinois. In Springfield." Herb crossed his right leg over the left and leaned back in his chair. "As of now, I'm not planning to check further, either."

"But what about Mark and the coin?"

"Well, I'm not sure. What we know about Harrington isn't a big help, is it?"

Gracie sighed, then leaned forward to tell Herb what Sally had told her about Mark's theory that if he could find more coins, he might be able to clear himself of suspicion.

"It's a good try, whether or not he finds anything," he agreed. "It could demonstrate his innocence — although, should he find another, there's always the possibility Miles will insist he must have taken more than one coin."

"Wouldn't that look more suspicious on Miles's part than on Mark's? Didn't he say he'd brought home only a few coins from the bank? Wouldn't he know if a second one was missing?"

"It would seem that way, wouldn't it?"

She tossed her head. "Well, I'm rooting for Mark."

"I know you are." He was smiling now. "And I appreciate your loyalty. Myself, I need to stay neutral, of course."

"Of course! But I can guess, I think, where your sympathies lay."

As Gracie got to her feet, Herb did likewise. "With a problem like this one," he said, "we need to view things from different perspectives, with multiple what-if's."

She agreed, but, being Gracie, she couldn't resist sending up a silent prayer that Mark's perspective prevail.

And she couldn't keep from adding a loving thought to strengthen Uncle Miltie's resolve as a lipreading companion. If he learned to tell jokes in sign language, that, too, might provide benefit for the greater community.

6

Gracie waited restlessly for her uncle's return. Not knowing just when that would be or even if he might have decided to eat lunch at the school, she'd decided on waiting before fixing anything.

It was after 12:45 when an unfamiliar tan car pulled up in front of her house. Uncle Miltie got out, then reached back in for his folded walker, which he opened and set up, all the time talking to the driver. He then closed the door and waved as the vehicle pulled away from the curb.

He looked buoyantly at her as she went onto the porch to greet him. "Your morning must have gone well."

"So much better than expected!" There was a sparkle in his bright blue eyes. "That Lynn is a little sweetheart! She and Sally certainly made me feel welcome. I was glad to be there, glad to be able to help."

"You're positively beaming."

And he was. It had seemed earlier as if he'd really needed his walker, leaning into it with each step. Now it was just something being pushed in front of him.

Why haven't I been aware of his reliance on his walker as a sign of anxiety, God? But then, that thought led to Gracie's turning her insight into a question about her own behavior. How do I unconsciously reveal my own unhappiness or stress?

The answer to that came instantaneously. *By talking things over with You, Lord, just like this. . . .*

"You know what?" Uncle Miltie was saying. "It turns out I wasn't a stranger to everyone. As soon as we got inside, Susan said to me, 'I brought my little sister to the library several times when you were there reading children's stories. We do read to her a whole lot, of course, but she loves sitting there on the carpet with all the other kids and listening to you.' "

He chuckled at the memory. "And, boy, did I work up an appetite!"

Gracie was already getting out the bread for sandwiches. She told him, "They get you without the jokes, so of course they love listening!"

She and her uncle both chuckled. He attempted to look indignant but failed. He was in too good a mood.

"We didn't get to even try much lipreading," he said as he watched her heat a container of frozen homemade pea soup, "but at least I can say 'hello' and 'goodbye' and a couple other things with finger spelling." He demonstrated these for Gracie, then asked, "Can you guess what they call doing this? It's *dactylology* — you know, from *dactyl,* meaning a finger or toe."

She smiled encouragement, and then he did something else with his hands, as he asked, "Want to guess what I just said to you?"

"I have no idea."

"I just said, 'I like you.' " He was proud of his prowess in a new arena, and Gracie was proud *of* him. "That's the sum total of what I've learned thus far — since I haven't yet found out how to say 'I love you,' I'll just repeat that last one a couple times, okay? For extra emphasis!"

He offered to help with the dishes, but as Gracie got to her feet she reminded him there were few dishes from a meal like this. "Go on in the other room and rest," she suggested. "You've had a big morning, and I'll bet you didn't sleep well last night, worrying about how it would go."

"Ah, Gracie, you know me too well." A delighted grin came to his face. "We're a good pair, looking out for each other the way we do."

She came around the table and leaned down to kiss his cheek. "I think I'm going to lie down now, too, and read. Then, when we're both refreshed, we can take a short walk together."

He looked at her with mock concern. "Only if you promise we won't go out Ferris Road."

She laughed. "It's a deal."

Gooseberry had obviously not been consulted about agreeing to rest for a while. He kept going to the screen door, his claws scratching noisily across the irregular metal at the bottom. "I know," Gracie told him. "I promise we'll head out later on."

She went into her bedroom and stretched out on top of the handmade quilt she used as a spread. Ah, it felt good to relax, even for a few minutes. . . .

She awoke, somewhat disoriented, to the ringing of her bedside phone. "Hello?"

"Grace Parks?"

The voice sounded somewhat familiar, but she couldn't place it. "This is she."

"Well, Mrs. Parks, I guess it's about time we talk."

She pushed herself up on her elbow. "Who is this?"

"Miles Stevens."

She was wide awake now, all senses alert as she sat up and swung her legs over the side of the bed.

"Hello, Miles, how are you?"

"What do you think you're doing, encouraging that young Canfield to . . ."

"*Mr.* Stevens," she interrupted firmly, "you called me in my own home, and I answered. However, neither courtesy nor hospitality requires my listening or responding to rude or arrogant messages. If or when you wish to call again, I shall expect an apology as well as a calm and businesslike conversation."

And she hung up.

All urge to sleep was gone.

She became more uncertain about whether she'd used the best tactic when seconds, then minutes passed. Finally, telling herself that a watched phone seldom rings, she went down into the kitchen for a glass of iced tea.

Still no call back.

Please, Lord, help me know what to say or do.

Well, she decided, I'm not going to just stand here like a lump of unleavened dough. She went to the utility closet for the broom. The kitchen floor could use some attention. There were cat hairs, bits of grass that must have stuck to her shoes or Uncle Miltie's, and about the usual amount of crumbs and spills.

She noticed several small spots near the sink and refrigerator, hardly enough to justify mopping the floor. Opening the top drawer to the right of the sink, she took from it a large rag, folded it once, dampened it under the faucet, then laid it on one of those spots. Placing her right shoe on that, she moved it back and forth several times, then went on to do the same with others.

Suddenly, in the midst of her floor-cleaning, she was remembering Elmo. Although they had loved one another dearly and did so much together, they had different tastes in many things, including books. El preferring science fiction for what he described as his escape from reality, and she, mysteries. He had loved to tease her about her habit of cutting paper towels into smaller squares to avoid waste, and she, in turn, had fondly mocked his inability ever to throw away even the most mended article of clothing. Your stitches make this old shirt more precious to me, he would tell her.

Gracie sighed, then shook her head in an effort to clear it. How do I let myself get into this state, this remembering? Over five years gone, and there are times like today when it seems as though he's just got to be coming home, walking in through that door.

There was a knock on the front door! From where she stood she could see through the sheer curtains that a man was standing there. For a split second she was filled with joy, for this man looked to be about as tall and well-built as her husband. But that moment of unrealistic, instantaneous happiness was replaced by a surge of awareness. El was not out on their — *her* — porch. He was not waiting for her to come greet him at the door.

Instead, awaiting her was a confrontation she dreaded, with Miles Stevens.

Her right hand felt cramped and, glancing down, she saw her fingers tightly gripping the back of the chair in which El used to sit. She was further brought back to reality by a second knocking, this time louder and lasting longer.

All right, she told herself, you are going to settle down and face him. She marched over to open her door and greeted him with a polite, "Hello, Miles."

He moved a step nearer, and she knew he was expecting to come into her house as he angrily informed her, "We were apparently cut off. . . ."

She pushed her shoulders back and her chin forward. She was ready for battle. He must have registered her stiffening, because his tone changed as he said, "Look, we need to talk about this."

She said nothing, just stood there looking at him through the screen door.

"Okay, I apologize for my — brusqueness, but you have to admit I have reason to resent your attitude."

She answered firmly, but still courteously, "As I have every reason to resent yours."

His eyebrows rose slightly. His mouth tightened. Then his face, without warning, relaxed into a large but definitely suspect grin. A grin that bordered on a smirk.

She suspected this might be just how he'd looked when he'd convinced Gracie's friend Marjorie Printz to believe he was doing her a wonderful favor when he paid her "twice the value" for her father's gold coins.

"Really, Gracie, this misunderstanding can be cleared up in no time at all if we just sit down and talk about it."

She knew she needed to allow herself to

listen to what he had to say. Unlocking the screen door, she stepped outside onto the porch and pushed the door closed. "Very well." She took a wicker armchair and indicated the one to her right for him to sit in.

He began with a statement that surprised her. "I understand you're quite fond of Mark."

"I've known him for a long time," she replied, "and have always been impressed by his character."

"But you do know that he's determined to save money to go to college. That's quite a sum."

"Yes, he's worked hard at mowing lawns and doing other jobs that don't interfere with his schoolwork. I find it commendable."

"I, too, appreciate that." He leaned forward a bit. "Mark has taken care of my yard both last year and this. He's always made a good job of it and that's why I trusted him. In fact, I even recommended him to many of my neighbors. That's why I find it so distressing that he took something very valuable that doesn't belong to him."

He was sounding quite reasonable. Gracie knew she had to make her argument carefully. "I understand you had a number of coins there on the table."

He nodded. "There were five."

"Were they all gold coins?"

He nodded. "Yes."

"Why did you have them there? Why did you bring them home, leaving behind the others at the bank?"

"What others?"

He stared at her.

"Are you saying those were the only gold coins you own?" she asked.

He gave a little laugh. "Really, Gracie, I understand your loyalty to a young man you like, but I do think just how many gold coins I possess is my own business."

She spoke deliberately, to control her rising anger. "I'm sure you must recall that it was you who brought up the subject in the first place. It was you who called me on the telephone and came here to my house to talk about the missing money. Since that's the case, I think my question's perfectly justified. How many gold coins do you own — and where are they?"

She felt that the retired banker now was on the defensive, although he answered smoothly, "I came to discuss one particular coin, and that's what I intend to do."

"I assume you have them insured, right? You have an inventory list for your records?"

"May I remind you again that that is no concern of yours?"

"And may I remind you that you're accusing Mark of stealing something though you won't offer proper proof that you ever owned it in the first place?"

"My entire career was in banking, Gracie Parks, as I think you well know. I have never before been accused of dishonesty."

Gracie spoke evenly. "And all my life has been spent with people, and I've learned a great deal about what makes them tick. Everyone has different motivations, and does things for many different reasons. So, Miles, what is your motivation for being here right now?"

He looked pained. "Folks here call you a helpful, loving person, the kind who always sees the best in people. So I came to you with the hope, the expectation that you'd be able to see reason. That you would want to help persuade that poor boy to stop his charade. This fable of his innocence is only that: a pretty story.

"You can't really want this to go to court, can you? Don't you realize that he'll be marked for life by the stigma of his thievery?" He pounded the arm of the white wicker chair with his fist, and his voice raised. "Is *this* how you prove your friendship?"

She got to her feet, and so did he.

"Come now, Gracie! You know you can't be certain that I'm not correct."

His voice and expression were now patronizing. She resented that, as well as everything that had preceded it. She even disliked the sound of her own name, hearing him speak it. The man was really too much.

"I think we'll have to agree to disagree," she told him. "And I think there's nothing more to discuss."

He took a step nearer, reaching out for her arm. "You're being unreasonable."

Suddenly they both heard the slam of a car door. Then came the sound of Herb's deep voice. The Willow Bend police chief strode up Gracie's front steps. "Good afternoon, my friends. Is there any trouble here?"

Miles Stevens shook his head. "No, no trouble at all, Herb. I just dropped by to talk with Gracie for a bit. We had a few things to discuss."

Gracie bit her lip.

Miles looked from one to the other, started to say something, then shrugged his shoulders, turned, and walked off the porch.

Neither Herb nor Gracie said a word until Miles's expensive black sedan had purred its way down the street. "Thanks, Herb," she told him. "Can I give you a cup of coffee?"

"Is it ready now?" he asked.

"It won't take long."

He glanced at his watch. "I'm expecting someone at my office in about fifteen minutes."

She opened the door as she reassured him, "I promise not to keep you more than ten, okay?"

"Sure."

"And in place of coffee, I do have iced tea," she offered, heading for the refrigerator.

He sat down at the table. "Well?" he said.

Gracie poured the tea and brought the glasses with her, talking all the while.

"I hung up on him this morning, which is one of the few times in my life that I've done that." She shrugged. "I guess I shouldn't have been surprised when he showed up here a little later."

"He's used to having his own way."

"But, Herb, what he wants is for me to talk Mark into giving up that coin, to hand it over to him."

"And you didn't agree to do that."

"No. It wouldn't be right."

"So what's the situation now?"

"The same as before, I guess. Except that he now knows for sure he can expect no help from me." She drew a long, slow breath. "Of course if it should end up that Mark did steal it, I'll owe Mr. Miles Stevens a great big apology."

"But I take it that, meanwhile, you're not losing sleep over that possibility."

She smiled. "For the time being, I'm resting well. But what might buy me a few extra hours of easy slumber is your telling me anything more you've learned about Clark Harrington."

"No luck there, Gracie," he said ruefully. "Sorry."

"Well, I know it's not for want of trying."

He nodded. "I've been making calls. But just don't have anything more that seems useful."

Gooseberry had come from the other room, and circled Herb's legs, rubbing against him. The policeman stooped to pet him, then walked outside with Gracie.

"What about Ohio, Herb? Or Illinois? You said he had connections there. . . ."

"I'm still waiting to hear. But I think if they had anything to tell me, I'd have heard by now."

She watched him drive off. Just as she was about to wave at a neighbor, she heard

Uncle Miltie's voice. "Gracie, who was the visitor?" he called.

She started toward him, smiling. "I just walked Herb to his car, and was thinking how blessed our town is to have someone like him looking out for our welfare."

"*Humph!* I never heard a sound, I'm sorry to say. I'd have liked to see him, too. Did he have anything to say about our coin controversy?"

"Not much — and he was only here a few minutes."

"What did he stop for? He's so busy, he doesn't seem to have much time for social calls."

She now filled him in about her earlier guest. His eyes widened.

"The thing is, I never knew Miles all that well before. Oh, I'd seen and spoken to him at all sorts of meetings and activities, but I'd never had a real conversation with him. And, you know, I just always had this sense he was sneaky. I can't explain it."

"Woman's intuition." He went over to the cookie jar, and took a molasses crisp she'd baked two days before. Taking a bite, he informed her, "You always manage to put the *cook* into cookie, Gracie, my girl."

"That's one of the many reasons I enjoy having you here. You don't take me and what I do for granted."

"Well, you have to admit that having a proper attitude keeps me well supplied with delicious treats."

She raised a fist. "Hey! I always thought your compliments were totally sincere."

"Uh oh!"

"Well, don't worry." She was heading out of the kitchen as she spoke. "I love baking, as you know, so you're going to be stuck with having home-baked goodies."

"Whew!" Uncle Miltie now reached into the cookie jar and grabbed a handful.

7

"Guess what, Gracie — the weatherman goofed for a change."

She hadn't really been paying attention since she had been busy going over, once again, the Sunday school lesson she'd be teaching in another two hours. "Which way did he err this time?"

"Much colder than predicted. Down to twenty-seven degrees, it says here." Uncle Miltie was checking the outdoor thermometer. When she didn't respond to that, he continued, "Poor old Fannie Mae has a white frosted roof and hood this morning."

"Well," she replied, still trying to keep her mind on the lesson, "then we'll need a few more minutes, won't we, in order to scrape windows?"

"They appear clear along this side — but

the front and back ones usually take more time."

"*Um-hmmm.*"

"And we mustn't forget the mums," he reminded her.

"*Um-hmmm.*"

"I like that big bouquet of mixed asters you fixed last night."

"*Um-hmmm.*"

There was a brief pause before, "I especially like those black and green ones."

"*Um-hmmm.*"

"Aha!" he cried. "I didn't think you were listening."

She looked up, questioning. "What?"

He snorted. "I've been talking away here and you kept saying, '*um-hmmm,*' as though you were actually listening. So I decided to trap you with some black asters!"

"Black asters?" Gracie laughed. "I'm no botanist but I'm pretty sure we don't have any like that, unless you somehow sneaked them in."

"You're safe on that count," he reassured her. "I just said that to see if you were paying any attention at all to your poor old uncle."

"I'm sorry." And she was. "But I do have to go over this lesson again."

"What's it about?"

He seemed to be missing the message that she still needed time for study. "I've read Acts more often than any other book in the Bible — except for the Gospels, of course — but the commentary for this lesson points out some interesting aspects about money, or the love of money, that is. It reminds us how mistaken we can be about what we think it can buy or give us."

"That is pretty appropriate right now," he commented.

"And it's nothing new! Here we have Ananias and Sapphira, for example" — she indicated Chapter 5 in her open Bible — "who were probably a well-intentioned couple who wanted to do good for the early church, and *did*.

"They sold property they owned, which may even have been passed down from generation to generation. They doubtless had the right to sell it if they wished, as it was also their right to do whatever they chose with the money received from it.

"They must have given far more than a tithe — or just a tenth — and those present when they brought it to the apostles must have been impressed and grateful. But the problem was their motivation. Their attempt to use the money in order to gain the esteem of others was wrong."

"Yeah, I remember when I first read that, I thought it seemed almost unjust of God to punish them when they were giving so much."

"Well, that's what's been troubling me — which angle to emphasize most strongly to the class. And then, once I'd decided it had to be motivation, that led me, again, into wondering about what's really going on in the minds of these three fellows — all so different — who are claiming the disputed coin."

Uncle Miltie lifted an eyebrow. "Well, Mark would undoubtedly say he hopes to be able to use the proceeds from the coin to help fund his college education."

"So the main question in his case is whether that desire of his could be strong enough that he'd actually steal in order to reach that goal."

Uncle Miltie nodded. "I'd guess Miles's motivation is simply the idea of possession, owning something valuable enough to make him feel privileged above others. People who collect such things are covetous . . . and tenacious."

"I got to thinking that I can relate to that," Gracie said unexpectedly. "It's sort of like that picture I have above the couch in the living room. It's an oil painting that

Elmo inherited, and people have often admired it, even offered to buy it were I to tire of it. But it's mine and I'm afraid that I'm proud to have it there where others can admire it and even hope to possess it."

Uncle Miltie didn't reply, only smiled.

"The only thing is, I at least am displaying this possession in public, not hoarding it secretly like Miles Stevens."

He patted her hand. "But neither of us can make even an uneducated guess as to our third contender's motivation."

Estelle Livett was waiting at the door of the Family Activity Center, her voice husky. "Make Barb listen, Gracie. I've told her that, with the antihistamine and the orange juice I've taken this morning, it's okay for me to sing those two brief solo parts in our anthem."

"I'm sure she doesn't want you straining your voice," Gracie soothed. "Remember last year about this time? Your allergies were acting up so badly you lost your voice entirely after singing that Sunday. . . ."

"I had a cold then, not just allergies."

"Whatever it was, you ended up unable to sing at all until after Thanksgiving, when we were well into our Advent and Christmas anthems." She put her hand on her friend's amply rounded shoulder. "Barb just doesn't want to risk not having your lovely soprano voice to count on this fall."

"I'll bet she's already asked Amy to sing my part!"

Gracie laughed. "As I recall, you had the chance to sing her part last summer for a similar reason. That's one of the good things about our choir. We do have backups."

Unfortunately, this innocent comment led to Estelle's stopping to extoll the marvels of the *very* large and wonderful choir back east in which she had sung long ago.

One of the things Gracie most appreciated about her vantage point from the choir loft was getting to see who was in church. This was especially true when it came to latecomers. Among them today was Rocky, who arrived while everyone was singing the second verse of the first hymn. Looking in her direction, he gave an unobtrusive thumbs-up as he took an aisle seat near the back.

He was an "occasional" attendee, at best, so it crossed her mind to wonder exactly why he had chosen this service. It didn't matter, though, she was simply grateful he had chosen to be here today.

She always enjoyed Pastor Paul's children's sermons, with all the kids coming forward to sit in the front seats. Today's topic was "Making Choices." After Paul had greeted them, he picked up a baseball bat from among some items placed at the end of the pew, then asked, "What is this?" Almost all of them answered correctly, as they also did when he held up a shuttlecock.

"Let's play badminton, Eric," he said to an intently listening six-year-old. Tossing the shuttlecock upward, he took a mighty swing with the bat, slashing at the light-weight feathered cone. One part shattered, drifting down to the floor, while the heavier, plastic covered nose-portion flew quite a distance.

Several children looked upset. Others giggled. Paul leaned down and picked up a part of the broken object and examined it. "*Hmmm,* something seems wrong here."

Eric had chased after the other half in the aisle. Now, bringing it to the pastor, he said, "You're supposed to use a *racket* for badminton."

"You know, you're exactly right." Paul reached for one of those, but also lifted a basketball, tossed it into the air, and used the racket to propel it gently into the lap of a nearby girl.

Eric reached for the basketball and handed it back to him, patiently explaining,

114

"You don't use a racket with a basketball. You use your *hands.*"

"You're right again, Eric." He smiled down at the youngsters. "And I appreciate your patiently explaining my errors — not yelling at me or anything, just giving me the right advice as to how to improve."

And then, taking a single step backward in order to include the whole congregation in what he was saying to the children, he elaborated on his theme — which was the need to choose the right actions and words when dealing with others.

". . . Because if we don't, we can hurt the feelings of people we care about, or even people we don't, and make them sad. Or," he picked up more pieces of the broken shuttlecock, "what's even more harmful is that we can even break their spirit — making them afraid to trust *any*one again.

"And we wouldn't want that to happen to anyone, would we?" he asked. His congregants murmured their understanding, although a few of the littler ones seemed more interested in the broken shuttlecock, which he then set carefully down.

One of the smallest girls saw her opportunity. As Paul remounted the pulpit, she followed him, tugging at the sleeve of his robe. "Here, Pastor Paul. Here's your shuttlecock. I'm sorry it's all broken."

He reached down to receive her gift. "Thank you, Angela, for bringing this to me, and for your concern. I truly appreciate it."

From where Gracie was sitting, she was almost sure there was moisture in Paul's eyes as his gaze for a moment remained on the file of youngsters now proceeding out of the sanctuary.

But then he cleared his throat and quoted, "And a little child shall lead them . . . ."

Paul should have children of his own — a wife and family. Gracie had thought that many times, and now again, she knew it was so. *He's such a loving person, and the little ones respond to that, as do so many of us — of all ages. Couldn't You arrange for him to find just the right life partner, Lord? Everyone who worships You here at Eternal Hope Community Church would sing Your praises even more loudly than usual!*

It was after the benediction that Uncle Miltie came up to her. "Hey, Gracie, how about our going over to the deli right away — maybe beat the crowd?"

"Sounds good to me. Rocky's here and you know he'll want to join us."

"Here he comes."

As they arrived at Abe Wasserman's well-

116

loved local institution, Uncle Miltie said, as he always did, "*Hmmm,* smell that! Nothing finer than a diner!"

Rocky corrected him. "You ungrateful wretch, you've got Gracie's cooking to inhale every day!"

Gracie laughed. "Not all these wonderful aromas on any one day."

He started to respond, but Abe was welcoming them. Gracie gave him a hug. Abe beamed. Gracie was a special favorite of his. Abe now motioned to an empty table, but Gracie shook her head. Abe had an odd expression on his face.

"The way I figure," Uncle Miltie was saying, "is that she's the performer and I'm the audience. All I have to do is make sure she never gets tired of encores!"

As Gracie started to sit down at their regular table, Rocky suggested, "How about the booth in the corner? It's quieter, and you know sometimes it's nicer to eat our scrambled eggs with salami and blintzes with sour cream and applesauce without my having to share you with everybody who needs your advice or wants to discuss a recipe. . . ."

"Well, Gracie is popular," Abe agreed. "But so is Willow Bend's esteemed newspaper proprietor!"

He beckoned to Amy, who'd also just arrived, to bring over tea and coffee and take their orders. Before heading back to the kitchen, however, he said in a low voice, "I couldn't tell you while we were standing back there, or while Amy was nearby, but I'd been trying to steer you in the vicinity of that young guy sitting over there."

Gracie now examined from a distance the profile of a slender, dark-haired man who seemed to be about thirty years old. "I don't think I know him, Abe. Should I?"

"Probably not. Yet."

"Yet?"

"His name's Clark Harrington."

"Oh. I see now."

Rocky exclaimed, "Our third contender for the double eagle!"

After Abe left them, Rocky mused, "I wonder how well Abe's gotten to know him. He didn't say if Harrington's been coming in regularly." He stood up.

"Come to think of it, I should probably go wash my hands before eating." Rocky grinned as he sauntered off.

Gracie smiled as she watched him move purposefully between tables and stop near the stranger. She had no way of knowing what was said, but Clark Harrington seemed not to resent the intrusion on his meal.

Rocky then stopped again for a few moments to speak with the stranger on his way back to the table where Gracie and Uncle Miltie were ignoring their food as they eagerly awaited his report.

"Seems like a friendly chap," he commented. "He says he's updating the computer system and computer labs at the high school, and will probably stay at Cordelia's for another week or so."

"Good work, Rocky." Gracie was thoughtfully considering what she'd just heard. "Does he know you're the editor of your paper?"

"Yep, he does. That's how I explained my curiosity."

"So what else did you learn?" her uncle asked impatiently.

"Well, he likes the town and is comfortable enough at Cordelia's and thinks we have a good school." He paused to look each of them in the eye. "And no, neither of us mentioned a gold coin."

"Does he seem, ah . . . sincere or open or — oh, you know what I mean."

He shrugged. "I'm not clairvoyant enough to gain that kind of insight in only a few minutes. I wish I were."

"Well, I thought maybe with your newsman's instincts, you might have made an educated guess."

He took a bite of scrambled egg before responding, "All I can say about Clark Harrington right now is that he appears to be friendly and straightforward."

Uncle Miltie was getting bored. No new facts — and he was still hungry. "You two ordering anything else?"

"Is that shorthand for 'Let's have some cheesecake?' "

"Your newspaperman's nose must be working now! I guess you saw the blackberry one on the counter as we came in!"

"And the cherry, too," the editor answered modestly.

Gracie laughed. "I'm too full," she told them.

"Not us!" her menfolk responded. "Amy!"

The teenager brought her pad and pencil to their table. "That's what I like — patrons who are easy to keep happy."

Amy giggled. Then a cloud crossed her face.

Gracie sensed something wrong. "You've had a bad experience recently?"

"Well, sort of." Amy glanced around.

"Tell me about it."

Amy shook her head. "I must get on the ball. I'll have your cheesecake for you in just a moment."

Gracie began to watch the girl as she went about her work. Was she avoiding Clark Harrington? It was hard to tell.

Still, Gracie thought she could see her intentionally walk around another table so she'd be approaching his from the far side when offering a beverage refill.

What did it mean? When Gracie got the chance, she quietly asked, "Has Clark done something to offend you, dear?"

Amy looked startled. "I'd — hoped it didn't show, and that Abe doesn't realize it."

Rocky now leaned forward. "What's he done? Harrington, I mean."

"Nothing, really. But he knows I'm Mark's friend and about our picking up trash that Saturday. So he's been making small talk to me about it when he comes in."

Amy hesitated. "That's probably why it bothers me, plus he's been hinting that he'd like to take me out."

Gracie was purposely calm. She didn't want to upset her young friend in any way. "You're a very attractive young woman. He should, though, have enough common sense to know how inappropriate that would be. He's too old, he's a stranger, and you would have given him no encouragement, I'm sure."

Amy looked at Gracie with gratitude.

"I'm just trying to do my job. So I've tried to stay polite."

Gracie reassured her, "Being courteous isn't any kind of invitation."

"I'd like to think that was right," Amy said anxiously. "But I'm kind of worried that he might have followed me home last night."

"What did you do?" Rocky asked, looking grim.

"I deliberately drove back out to Main Street, and stopped right under the light there at the Willow Mart. I went inside just long enough to buy a magazine, staying up front so I could watch my car."

"And the other car?"

"I'm not very good at recognizing them. I can't really tell the difference." She looked apologetic now. "But some car I didn't know followed me."

Gracie prompted, "Followed you to your house?"

"Thank goodness I have one of those electronic garage-openers, so I drove right in, and closed it behind me."

"And you didn't tell your folks?" Uncle Miltie demanded.

"The thing is, I'm just not positive about it. If it turns out to have been a coincidence that a car stayed behind mine, I don't want to get anyone in trouble."

"You really must tell your folks, dear."

"I don't want to bother them with worries that might be my imagination." She looked uncomfortable. "I shouldn't have mentioned this to you."

Gracie disagreed. "Yes, dear, you should. We're your friends, you know. And your parents are your friends, too."

Amy sighed. "I must get back to work."

Rocky stopped her. "First of all, you must tell Herb. Do it right away."

She shook her head. "I can't, not now."

"Then I'm going to, my dear. You're far too precious to us to let anything happen."

"Please don't!" She looked panicked. "I knew I should never have burdened you with this, but. . . ."

Gracie now asked, "What time are you finished?"

"Not until five-thirty."

"And you walked over from church?"

"Yes, but. . . ."

"I'll be here at 5:35," she promised. "Don't leave until I get here, okay?"

Seeing Amy's face, Gracie fished in her purse for the small pack of tissues she always kept there, and handed it to the anxious girl.

Amy accepted it gratefully.

8

From Abe's deli, Gracie, Uncle Miltie and Rocky headed directly to the police station. But Herb Bower wasn't there. Gracie then tried to contact him on his cell phone but, after leaving a message, had to wait an hour before he responded to her S.O.S.

"What's up, Gracie?"

"Maybe nothing, Herb, but still I wanted to run it by you."

"Well, you've got my full attention now."

She briefly told of her concerns. At the end, he asked, "Did you chat at all with Clark Harrington?"

"No. But I trust Amy when she says there's something about him that makes her uncomfortable."

"Hmmm."

"Have you found out anything more

about him yet?"

"No."

"Well, that may be good news."

"Yes," he agreed. "But it still won't hurt for both of us to keep an eye on him."

"My feelings exactly!"

Gracie now felt restless, so she invited Gooseberry for a walk.

He looked up at her from the carpet, stretched, then meandered to the kitchen, for all the world as though he was deigning to do her a favor. She laughed. "You can't fool me! You want to go out every bit as much as I do!"

She'd already let him out when she remembered to scribble a note, "Back soon — we've gone for a walk," which she laid on the kitchen table. Looking at the door, she crossed the porch and went down the steps. Gooseberry had been rather impatiently pacing but now, after a brief, wide-eyed stare which his mistress interpreted as "It's about time you got here!" he stalked down the sidewalk, head and tail held high.

"Okay, kiddo," she told him, "you map our route today. If you stay within reasonable bounds, you can determine where we go and when we return."

He continued walking ahead of her, not even looking around to make sure she was following. He did, however, wait each time she briefly stopped to speak to people enjoying the lovely afternoon.

"Did you know from the beginning that we were headed for Ferris Road?" she asked as they got there. "Are you feeling your sleuthing bones acting up? Or do I mean whiskers?"

Gracie wished she had thought to bring a camera, since the leaves were glorious in all their autumn color. She'd walked quite a ways when she saw someone step out onto the road from a side lane. The moment he saw her, he ducked back and a second later she heard a car door closing.

Suddenly, he emerged out onto the road again. It was only then that she realized who it was. "Mark!" she called, "Hi!"

He waved, also. "Hi, Mrs. Parks!"

"Have you found anything with that metal detector?"

For a split second he looked startled. "Metal detector?"

"The one your mother told me you'd been using out here, the one you must have just put in the car." Gracie didn't wish to seem like she was checking up on him. At the same time, she wanted to hear his version of his actions.

She at first thought he was going to deny

it, but then he said, "You know I found that double eagle. You were with me."

"But what about after that?"

He looked sulky. "Well, I *did* find one more," he told her reluctantly.

"One more what?"

He still hesitated. "An eagle, a ten-dollar coin. Two days ago."

"My goodness! Your hunch was correct then!"

"That's right." Mark suddenly looked pleased. "I thought there might be others and there were. At least this one. I tried to get a book giving current values, and found a place on the Internet where they offer coins for sale. Since my eagle's one of a fairly small minting, and not too many are known to have survived, it's worth a lot, too."

"Oh, my!" Gracie didn't know what to say.

"What's Miles Stevens going to say about this, huh?"

"Well, they almost have to be from somebody's private collection, if not his, don't they?" Gracie mused. "But from whose? And how did anything this valuable come to be here, of all places?"

"I keep wondering, too. Isn't it interesting that nobody's ever mentioned this second one? But," he was frowning, "nobody ever mentioned the double eagle, either, not until after I found it."

She looked around at all the trampled-down growth. "Where did you find your eagle, Mark?"

"Right over there," he said, pointing to some thick undergrowth. He stopped her from moving nearer. "Be careful, Gracie! That's poison ivy!"

"Oh!" She shivered. "It sure is!"

"Is that why you bought your metal detector?"

"Well, yes. I'm allergic to poison ivy, so I couldn't go pawing around through all these leaves. I figured that if I wore boots, like today," he said, sticking one foot out toward her, "and poked around with the detector, if it told me something was there, then I could put on the long, heavy plastic gloves and find what was making it act that way."

"So that's how you found the new coin!"

"*Um-hmmm.* And that's of course why I'm here again this afternoon, hoping I might find yet another!"

Gooseberry had been unusually patient with Gracie's staying in one place for so long. Now, however, he was circling her ankles and edging toward the road. He stopped there, looking back to check whether or not she was obeying his instructions.

As she and Gooseberry started back the way they'd come, she turned around to call, "You do have that in a safe place, don't you, Mark?"

"I — hope so."

She took a couple steps back toward him. "Might it be a good idea to put it with the other one?"

"Probably — but I didn't want to bother him."

"He was the one to make the offer before," she reminded him.

"Yeah, but . . ."

"So how about my asking him about it?"

"Well, I suppose you could. You're good friends, aren't you?"

"Yes, we are. And his wife sings with me in the choir." She was nearly back to him when she asked, "You don't happen to have it with you now, do you?"

"Well," with what appeared to be a sheepish grin, he said, "it just so happens that I do."

She resisted the impulse to scold him, telling him how unwise that was. Instead she merely said, "How about driving us back to town? If Herb's at the station, we could get it taken care of right away."

He agreed. Then, at the edge of town, he asked, "You didn't get a call from Mom today, did you?" He looked worried.

She shook her head. "No. Do you know what she wanted to talk about?"

"Well, she may have to give up her Sunday school class."

She turned to stare at him. "She does such a good job with those children. It would be a shame."

He shifted a bit on the seat. "She thinks maybe she'd better, since she got that letter."

"What letter?"

"Oh." There was a pause before he went on. "I maybe — should let her tell you."

"All right." Gracie knew she needed to be patient.

He exhaled completely, and pushed his fingers through his thick, dark brown hair. "It was on the screen door this morning, folded over once and fastened there with tape."

It was all she could do to keep from asking questions, but she waited, hoping he'd go on, which he finally did. "It was written in funny letters on regular white computer paper, and it wasn't very pleasant. What it said was that she's not fit to be a teacher of any sort and if she doesn't voluntarily give it up, then there's going to be trouble. I right away thought it meant her work with Lynn, but Mom feels it's about the church and her Sunday school class."

"There was nothing else?"

"Well, nothing that's going to be of any help."

"Would you be willing to tell me what it is?"

He looked even more uncomfortable than before. "Mom says it's a Bible verse from somewhere in Matthew, though I don't remember where. It goes something like, 'Outwardly you appear righteous to people, but inwardly you're full of lawlessness.' "

Gracie looked fiercely indignant. One question remained. "Was the note handwritten? You said 'funny letters.' "

He was keeping his eyes on the fairly empty street. "It was a computer-generated font."

They were approaching the station, so she suggested, "Perhaps you should mention this to Herb."

He was giving his full attention to turning into the parking lot. "Isn't Mom the one to do that — if she wants to?"

She knew he was more worried than he was showing. But he was also being sensitive to his mother's feelings.

"You're right, of course. I'd probably be

upset if Arlen or anyone else went over my head like that." She sighed. "I do hope, though, that you can get her to talk with Herb or with Paul. Or even me."

They walked together up the slanted ramp to the door and went inside, Gooseberry again marching, head and tail high, through the short hallway. Gracie turned toward Herb as he came out to greet them, "He's come to turn himself in," Gracie announced.

The police chief bent to stroke the large orange cat between his ears and along his back. "Mouse murder, I suppose," Herb replied. "You can be sure I'll get him the best defense attorney possible!"

Gracie laughed as she led the way inside his office and slid the chair beside his desk. "We're here to ask a favor."

He smiled at Mark. "Which is . . . ?"

"You already know about Mark's buying the metal detector."

Herb glanced toward him and nodded, and she went on, "Well, his search was rewarded. He's now found another gold coin, an eagle."

He reached across to shake hands. "Congratulations!"

"It was a long shot," Mark admitted.

Herb's glance shifted to hers for a

moment, then back to Mark, who was explaining his reasoning while taking the coin from his pocket and handing it across the desk. "Gracie says maybe this should stay with the first one, in your safe — if that's okay with you."

"Good idea. But whether or not it's kept here, I'd suggest your telling nobody else at this point — other than your mother, that is."

"I found it yesterday, and Mom and Gracie — and now you — are the only ones who know about it." He then asked anxiously, "You haven't had a report of anyone's missing it, have you?"

Herb shook his head, and Mark sank back into the chair, obviously relieved. "Then maybe there won't be so much conspiring this time, everyone trying to claim it."

Gracie sighed. "I sincerely hope not!"

Once again she and Mark signed papers stating that the coin was being placed under the protection of the chief of police. As Herb closed the safe's heavy door and turned the knob, he asked, "You're planning to continue searching for more?"

"Whenever I have the free time."

The two adults shook hands with Mark as he left the office. Then Gracie made her way home.

Gracie couldn't get the threatening letter Sally had received out of her mind throughout the evening. *What would I do if I received an anonymous message like that? Lord, I'm glad You have blessed me with friends and loved ones who have never tried to hide behind an unidentified threat. I believe it's just someone blustering, but there's no way to be sure. Help me to help Sally face this crisis. She surely has enough on her hands with Mark's situation.*

Everything she knew about Sally was positive. She'd been a loving, faithful wife and mother. It was her husband who'd taken himself out of the marriage, with hardly a look back at his wife, son or two daughters.

Thank goodness Sally had been able to keep the house! The child support payments she received were hardly enough to meet expenses, so she did have to work. She'd been in the beginning of her sophomore year in college when she got married, and when Mark, her first child, was born she'd dropped out. Therefore, despite her love of teaching, she didn't have her certification and could serve only as an aid.

During her first two years working in the school system she had served as the companion of a boy with severe physical and emotional problems. She'd loved and cared for Larry, and had been dismayed when his family decided to place him in an institution.

But then came Lynn. Sally had undergone special training to prepare for working with a hearing- and speech-impaired child, and was now with her for the fourth year. Everyone was delighted with the girl's progress and development.

What possible justification could there be for threatening to put a stop to *that?*

On the other hand, why would anyone want her to quit teaching her Sunday school class, if that's what the message meant?

Gracie recalled the short-lived furor when one of the older women in the church — one who'd never been married nor volunteered to teach a class in her life — decided that it wasn't "fitting for someone divorced to be teaching those innocent young children in Sunday school!"

Hattie Bomboy had threatened even to quit Eternal Hope Community Church if Sally wasn't removed from teaching. But, then again, she'd threatened that for years while trying to get her own way about a variety of issues.

She still hasn't left us. Unfortunately! Gracie thought wryly.

Might this be Hattie resuming her old crusade? If so, why? Could it be because of rumors concerning the ownership of Mark's coin? Was there any chance that she was a friend or relative of Miles?

Gracie decided she'd be much more concerned about that possibility if she could even remotely imagine that ornery octogenarian using a computer!

She didn't get up right away when awaking early the following morning. Instead, Gracie kept going over — as she often liked to do — small details of the celebration being hosted by Anna and Joe Searfoss. It was coming up so soon. But it looked to be a pretty straightforward catering job and it had the added appeal of being for the Searfosses, whom she adored.

She'd ordered the chicken when picking up those dozens of eggs, which she'd hardboiled yesterday. Uncle Miltie always enjoyed helping remove the shells, cracking each egg by lightly banging it against the sink, then rolling it between his palms. He frequently demanded Gracie's attention when he was able to get the entire shell off in one piece. "Who's the eggspert now?" he would crow.

The beets had come from their own

garden, for her uncle liked growing the green leaves of spinach and the red-veined leaves of beets among her many-hued flowers. And now the beets had been cooked, skinned, cut up and packed into large jars, along with the eggs, vinegar, seasonings and the dark red juice in which the beets had been cooked.

Other than this, however, nothing had actually been completed for the big day. Reaching for the tablet and pen she always kept in the drawer of her bedside table, she began jotting list after list of what was to be done, and by whom. To most people, this might seem a huge undertaking, but Gracie knew from experience that the individual or team heading each list could be relied upon.

Gracie picked up the annual *Daily Guideposts* devotional book, read the selection for the day, and spent time praying for her family, friends, church, town and nation. She closed with special prayers for Mark and for Sally, for Lynn and her family, for Marjorie Printz and the Searfosses, and for Clark Harrington and Miles Stevens, too. No one was beyond the reach of prayer.

And it was then that Gooseberry strolled into her room, meowing the message that it was time for his mistress to be up and around, facing the day ahead.

9

"Are . . . you . . . (something) . . . to . . . the (something) center . . . to-day." The studious frown left Uncle Miltie's face as he crowed, "I've got it, Gracie. You just asked, 'Are you going to the senior center today?' "

"That's great! You're coming along well with your lipreading."

". . . you're . . . coming along well . . . with your lipreading."

"Fantastic!"

"I didn't get that word, 'cause your mouth changes shape when you're laughing. Try something else."

"Okay, but just this one more time. Then you can take those plugs out of your ears!"

Grinning, he reached up and removed them, having obviously understood what she'd said, though not repeating it. "You know, Gracie, I've often been concerned about not always hearing as well as I should. But now I'm beginning to think I must have been doing some lipreading all along, and just didn't realize it."

"I wouldn't be surprised. It reminds me of Sally's saying how quickly Lynn took to it."

"I've got a whale of a lot more practicing to do before I'm anywhere near as proficient as she is."

"Of course. Just remember, though, you haven't been doing it very long." She transferred the breakfast dishes to the dishwasher and brought back with her both her cell phone and the paper on which she'd been working before getting out of bed. "And now I must make some calls for Sunday."

"Are you too busy to talk?" she asked Marge, having reached her at her shop. "I tried you at home first."

"I came in early."

"So what are you doing? Cleaning up?"

"Who, me?" She laughed, as did Gracie, who suspected the truth. "I have a new book from the library, and sitting here in the early morning is a surprisingly good way to get a bit of peace and quiet. No one's looking for me to be at work yet."

"Except me." Gracie smiled to herself.

"Is it a romance you took out?"

"What else?"

Gracie responded with, "I like them, too. I even don't mind if there's a romance in one of my mysteries."

"And I'm generous enough to admit that a mystery's acceptable in one of my romances, too."

They often passed on books they knew the other would like. Now they had a few new titles to recommend. But, suddenly, Marge changed the subject.

"Just one more thing — did you hear that Sally's giving up her Sunday school class? That might mean she'll have the time to come back to the choir, especially now that her daughters are older."

"Who told you that?" *Has Sally really given in to the demand, Lord? I was hoping she'd hold firm, knowing how You were holding her in Your love.*

"I heard it from Comfort. Rick found out last night when doing his ambulance duty."

"Was there an accident?" Gracie didn't remember the Volunteer Fire Company's sirens blowing. So she knew there hadn't been a fire.

"Not this time. Miles Stevens was having pain in his chest, and dialed 911. Rick was on call, but apparently didn't have to do much. They took Miles to the ER, though."

"Do you have any idea how Miles is now?"

"She said Rick checked this morning, before leaving for work. The hospital told him that tests didn't seem to indicate that he'd had a heart attack. He'll be back home later today."

Gracie put the phone down slowly, wondering if it had been Miles who, despite his own distress, had passed on the news of Sally's giving up her Sunday school class. On the other hand, it might have been someone else with the ambulance crew or there in the emergency room who'd mentioned it to Rick. The truth was, people in small towns were full of information and usually all too willing to share it.

She kept going over and over this small puzzle without feeling certain she'd arrived at any solution.

She found that she was grateful when Uncle Miltie came back to the kitchen to tell her he was ready to be off for his scheduled practice with Lynn.

Gracie stopped at church on her way home from taking him. In her care were boxes of foodstuffs to be used at the Searfoss dinner. Carrying in the first load, she found the church secretary in the

141

kitchen fixing herself a cup of tea. "Hi, Pat. How are things going?"

"Fine, thanks. What about you?"

"Great. I had to stop at the store for some stuff, so figured I might as well bring the potatoes in now, rather than unloading them twice, at home and here."

"Good idea. Is there more to be brought in?"

"Well, yes — but I can handle it."

"I'm sure you can, Gracie, but I'm going out with you anyway, and help carry."

As they returned with their arms filled, Gracie asked as casually as possible, "I didn't notice Paul's bike. Is he in his office?"

"He walked over this morning."

"Oh, Pat, didn't you once work with Miles Stevens? I just heard he was taken to the hospital by ambulance last night."

"Oh, dear! What's wrong?"

"Possible heart attack. But probably not. Do you know him well?"

"Does anyone?" Pat gave a wry smile. "When he was at the bank, he always seemed to be so — I don't know — sort of officious and pretentious or something. I was never that comfortable around him."

Gracie now had her supplies stacked neatly in a corner of the big kitchen. "I think

I'll go pester your boss for a few minutes," she said to Pat Allen.

She found Paul seated at his desk, a picture of concentration as he studied his computer screen.

She cleared her throat to get his attention, and the young pastor glanced up, a smile lighting his face as he rose from his desk chair. "Good morning, Gracie. And welcome."

She slid her hands into his outstretched ones. "I'd brought some things to the kitchen, and thought I'd stop in to talk with you."

"I'd have been sad if you hadn't."

"You looked totally engrossed."

"I'm never too busy to see you."

She did believe him. That was one reason she usually made the effort to not take too much advantage of his generosity when it came to sharing her thoughts with him. "There are several things I thought I should mention. Just stop me if you already know them," she began.

He nodded encouragement. She began by telling him about her conversation with Mark, then about those with Herb and Marge. "May I ask, Paul, if Sally's said anything to you about giving up her class?"

"No, she hasn't — and I hope she doesn't!

Those kids really do love and respect her!"

"What's your feeling about the anonymous note? Who might have written it?"

"I'm as unwilling to make a guess as I think you are."

"Is it probable, or even possible that the writer might have been referring to Sally's work with Lynn, instead of her teaching here?"

"I don't feel I have enough information even to make a guess."

"*Hmmm.* It would have been so easy to write a clearly understandable message that its not being done raises the question as to whether the ambiguity was accidental or deliberate."

"Sally's kept the paper, hasn't she?"

"I didn't ask. One's impulse, I think, would be to throw away such a thing instantly. However, if you're thinking of fingerprints or anything, they'd undoubtedly be badly smudged by now."

"Well, I'm no FBI lab technician."

"Neither am I. But maybe I could go see her after school. Just talk to her to let her know she's not alone. We all need to know that. And, of course, we never are."

Paul smiled. "Your faith is one of the things I love most about you, Gracie."

He leaned back in his chair, then said unexpectedly, "How would you feel if you were Sally?"

"I hope I'd appreciate knowing I had a friend on whom I could rely. But I'd also appreciate all the tact and sensitivity that that friend could muster."

"I think that says it all," Paul said, looking at her with an approving expression. "God bless you, Gracie Parks."

She blushed.

They went on briefly to discuss Mark's situation and Miles's stubbornness, but she didn't tell Paul about Mark's discovery of the second gold coin. Don't feel too proud of yourself for keeping one little secret, she reminded herself. You've told him just about everything else.

She got up from her chair. "I hate even to suggest it, but is it possible that someone knows something else about Sally, or thinks he does, and is using that against her?"

He stood up also. "I can't imagine what it could be."

"Me, neither, dear friend. Me, neither."

At home Gracie was still distracted. She got out the sweeper and sought out some of Gooseberry's favorite spots. He'd know them again even without the fluffy markings, that was certain. What she needed right then was something to keep her busy, something that required little concentration.

It was late in the afternoon when she decided to call her niece Carter Stephens in Chicago. She was a lawyer whose job was in the district attorney's office. The phone rang five times before being picked up by a man. "This is James Riley, a colleague of Miss Stephens. She's unable to come to the phone right now, but perhaps I can take a message?"

"Hello, Jim Riley," she greeted the familiar voice. "This is Carter's Aunt Gracie from Willow Bend, Indiana."

"Well, hello to you, Gracie Parks from Willow Bend, Indiana."

She laughed. "What a memory!"

"What an aunt our Carter has! She's kept us up-to-date with all your local mysteries. We have cases far less interesting around here, I promise you."

"Willow Bend's a real crime capital," she agreed, then heard a chuckle from the other end of the line. She went on, "I'm in something of a quandary right now, and thought perhaps Carter might have some ideas that could help."

"She's tied up with a big court case just now, and probably won't be back at all today. If she is, it will be rather late. Would you like me to leave a message for her to call you as soon as possible?"

"Thanks, Jim, I'd appreciate that."

"No problem. Look, I'm not trying to interfere if this is something related to family or anything. But if there's anything I can do to be of any use, I'd be glad to try."

"I appreciate that. And I'm going to take you up on it." She said thankfully to herself, I can see why Carter says Jim's like a second father to her, or a dear uncle.

Briefly she told him about the coin and the two men who were trying to claim it.

Jim said, "So tell me again, what do you know about this Clark Harrington?"

"He's apparently a computer expert. The trouble is, nobody seems to know anything else for sure about him. Our chief of police . . ."

"Ah, yes. How is Herb?"

"You don't forget anything, do you?" She laughed. "Herb's just fine." But then she became serious again. "He actually checked with someone in Illinois who said Clark's record was a tiny bit iffy — but not enough to make him persona non grata here in Willow Bend."

"Well, how about giving me a little more to go on, Gracie? What's he look like and how old is he, where does he live and/or work? Whatever you can think of."

She was almost embarrassed to admit how little she had to give him. But Jim just told her he happened to have some time right now to follow up on a few things which, from his perspective, could turn out to be most interesting.

Gracie hung up, feeling somewhat relieved but also worried if there was something else she should be doing. Suddenly it occurred to her. She and Gooseberry could take a walk in the direction of Cordelia Fountain's. The redoubtable tourist home proprietor was pretty observant and might have noticed something she'd be eager to report.

But, after her visit with Cordelia, Gracie was no more enlightened than she had been. Cordelia had been the one first to bring up the subject of Clark Harrington. According to her, her boarder was "such a nice young man, so gentlemanly and quiet." She added, "You'd never know he was in the house if you didn't see him come in, or notice the bit of light showing under his door at night."

"Aren't you ever a little nervous, Cordelia?"

"Not at all." She laughed. "I've run this place for well over a quarter-century, and

148

never lost so much as a bath towel."

"Does he use your phone much?"

"Not at all. He explained when he first came that he'd be using his cell phone to make business and other calls."

"That's good, especially if he's going to be here a long time."

"Well, he told me that his work at the school, his updating computers and putting in new things, should be finished in seven to ten days of actual work — and *that* was almost two weeks ago."

Gracie tried to get the wording of her next question just right. "Since he evidently goes from place to place to work, I wonder if he has mail forwarded?"

Cordelia informed her, "He has his laptop computer with him, so he relies on e-mail."

"Has he mentioned a wife and children?"

"No. And I haven't asked."

Gracie felt stymied. What to try now? The good news was that the one message on her answering machine when she got home turned out to be from Jim Riley, as she'd hoped.

"Greetings to you, Inspector Gracie. This is your humble deputy checking in. Here's what I've learned thus far about Mr. X. The address you gave me for his employer is that of a mailing service, one of those businesses that, for a fee, provides a 'mailbox' along with your personal box-number. I haven't given up, mind you, but that's all the time I have for this project today. Perhaps your highly efficient niece will have the opportunity to do better. Good-bye for now."

"Hmmph!"

Gracie was standing there staring at the machine when Uncle Miltie interrupted her thoughts. "I thought I heard voices. What's going on?"

"That's a very good question." She turned to face him. "But I don't have a good answer."

He frowned, perplexed. "What's that supposed to mean?"

"I wish I knew!"

"C'mon, Gracie, out with it!"

"Okay, but have a seat here at the table while I get us each a glass of water."

Sitting down across from him, she told how she'd reached Jim Riley when trying to find Carter, and then of his phoning her back. "Doesn't it seem strange to you that Clark's so — secretive?"

"Most people don't go around broadcasting their business, you know."

"Well, he's not so reticent that he isn't demanding that Mark give up that double eagle!"

"He's not going to get it, is he?"

"Not if I can help it!"

The phone rang, and Gracie hurried to answer it, hoping it would be Carter. It wasn't, but it was a caller she could cheerfully greet. "It's good to hear from you, Anna. I hope you're not anxious about Sunday's dinner."

"No, dear," Anna Searfoss reassured her. "At least I hope I don't need to be. You remember, of course, that we didn't send out invitations, saying only that anyone from church was welcome to come, as well as any of our other friends who wanted to.

"But we are trying to keep track of just who's planning to come. I think it's going to be a lot of people!"

Gracie was confident of her planning abilities. "We've made arrangements to feed at least a thousand people," she teased.

"The multitudes, I guess," Anna responded affectionately.

"You've got it. I've been meaning to call you about something else, dear. I know you asked Sally to bake the cake. . . ."

"She *offered* to make and decorate a big sheet cake, and I said I'd appreciate it — and I do. But," now Anna's voice sounded troubled, "will that be enough?"

"Several of the women are already planning to bring extras, including two large frosted cakes. I'll talk with Sally after she gets home from school today. If she thinks we might need more, I'll ask around for another volunteer, or maybe bake a couple myself."

"But you have so much else to do right now, Gracie! With Joe's help, I can mix up a package-cake or two."

"Well, don't buy the cake mix or ingredients until you hear from me, Anna," Gracie suggested. "I'm almost sure Sally and I will decide we have plenty."

But as she headed home, Gracie was mentally going over the rest of the menu. Yes, she'd better order more chicken thighs and split breasts. And she'd pick up another large seedless watermelon, as well as more honeydews and cantaloupes.

You could never have too much, she knew, because whatever was left would be joyously shared with those who would most appreciate the bounty.

10

Gracie had gone out to help Uncle Miltie with the flower beds and was on her knees pulling weeds from the narrow bed alongside the garage when a car pulled into the driveway.

"Hey, George, how about going with us to the senior center for some pinochle?" It was Lou Simpson, Willow Bend's retired police chief, and Joe Searfoss.

"We-e-ll, I should finish this dead-heading." Uncle Miltie stood there looking at the difference between the flowers to his left, which already had their spent blooms removed, and those yet to be trimmed. "You know it's a jailable offense to let all the plant's energy go into producing seeds instead of more flowers."

Lou laughed. "You're right. I'd have thrown the book at you!"

Gracie looked up at her uncle, knowing how much he enjoyed the fellowship of the men. "I doubt it will make much difference if you trim them now or this evening when it's cooler. For that matter, I'm going in fairly soon myself. The temperature must have risen at least a dozen degrees since we came out."

His face lit up, though he wouldn't admit that he was pleased with this reasoning. "You're right about that, Gracie." He raised his arm in order to wipe his forehead on the sleeve of his shirt, then reached for his walker, which was parked behind him. "Tell you what, fellows, give me a minute or two to wash up, and I'll be with you."

The two men got out of the car to keep Gracie company as her uncle hurried back to the porch steps. She noted that he wasn't leaning on the walker at all, just pushing it ahead of himself. He did, though, use the sturdy handrail as he went up the steps.

Lou observed, "He seems to be getting along better this summer, doesn't he?"

"Yes, he is — actually. But he's usually better in the summer. It's partly because of the heat, but he's also more active physically, and outside a lot more, working here in the garden and helping with the yard trimming."

Joe now cleared his throat. Looking at Gracie with affection, he said, "Anna and I sure appreciate all the work you're doing for our party."

She smiled at him. "It's fun doing it for people like you."

"Like us?"

"Sure." She got to her feet. "I like engineering a meal for the people I care about. Friends and feasts go together. And it's even nicer when those friends are so easy to work with."

"Do you have many who are — ah — disagreeable or grumpy?"

"More than you'd expect — although each party tends to have a different version of any transaction," she admitted. "You two told me what you wanted, and that's what you're getting. There are always some who keep changing their minds from day to day, or have to have every single detail spelled out. Then they lean over my shoulder all the time, making sure I'm doing the right thing at the right time in the right way."

He frowned thoughtfully. "I couldn't handle that kind of pressure, Gracie — and you shouldn't have to, either!"

"You sound like Elmo," she replied, but she was smiling. "My dear husband sometimes got even more upset than I did when that happened, and was quite disturbed with me on several occasions — as well as with the troublemaker."

"I can see why!"

"I assured him, however, that I really did have the upper hand. I could stand someone's being difficult one time — but there was no way I'd do a repeat catering job for that person!"

He appeared about to say something, then switched to a different subject. "Who do you think is the rightful owner of that double eagle, Gracie?"

"Are you interested in what I can prove? Or in my female intuition?" she teased.

He grinned. "Your sleuthing abilities undoubtedly have more to do with the latter. It was Lou, when he was police chief, and now Herb, who have to do the proving."

His friend chuckled.

"Well, I was out there picking up trash with Mark at the time he found it, Joe, and I doubt *very* much that he was faking his surprise — or his sense of gratitude for the possible bounty it could bring him."

"He's always seemed like a good kid, and an honest one. I'm hoping he gets to keep that coin."

Joe had lived here all his life, so this

seemed a good opportunity for Gracie to ask, "Miles is a native Willow Bender, right?" Lou and Joe both nodded.

"Yep, he was born here, and as far as I know the only time he's been away much was when he left for college, in New England somewhere. He and Hattie both went there." Joe looked to Lou for confirmation.

"Hattie Bomboy?" That was the only Hattie she knew. "Are they related?"

"Step-brother and –sister. His mom died when he was real little, and his dad married Hattie's mother maybe two or three years later." This was Lou's contribution.

"Oh."

"Why did you ask?"

"Well, you mentioned that both of them went East to college, so I wondered if there was some connection. . . ."

Uncle Miltie was now coming back out onto the porch, so even-tempered Joe just added, "And they both have something of the same dour disposition, don't they?" Gracie looked at him thoughtfully.

Lou and Joe then waited for their friend as they started back to Lou's car. "Let's go, George!"

Gracie bent to pick up her uncle's extra clippers and decided to trim the two butterfly bushes before going inside. They'd been blooming profusely for weeks but now were rather raggedy with their long brownish seed-spikes protruding.

It was nice of the men to come for Uncle Miltie, she thought. Actually, he had made many good friends here in Willow Bend and, though he sometimes spoke nostalgically about friends in his old hometown, he'd made little effort to keep in touch.

She found herself humming a tune she didn't at first recognize, one that had a pleasant meter and rhythm. Oh, yes, now she knew — it was one that Barb had included in an informal program back in June. It had something to do with friendship, or having friends. Gracie hummed through it, trying to recall some of the rather simple but affective words.

Sometimes — usually! — simplicity made for the most meaningful expression of any sentiment, Gracie thought. That was because it allowed your own heart and spirit to supply the emotion.

There were a lot of lines ending with rhymes to *friend,* like *mend* and *send* and even two-syllable ones like *amend.*

As she continued working on the second of the tall butterfly bushes, some of those almost-forgotten words started to come back.

> "When you're lonely, need a friend,
> Someone on whom to depend,
> Reach out to your neighbor in your
>   pew.
> Do not be too proud or shy,
> Look at others in the eye,
> Maybe they've been longing to know
>   you."

Gracie knew that wasn't exactly right, especially those last two lines, though they didn't sound so off when sung. There were several other verses, yet they continued hovering elusively just out of reach somewhere in the recesses of her mind. However, the last three lines of the final verse she remembered well, so she hummed, then sang them to herself here in her yard:

> "I know if at life's end
> I should die without a friend,
> I'd be the poorest person in the land."

Thank You, God, for my many wonderful friends. I don't know how I could get along without them — and that goes especially for Uncle Miltie, whom I originally invited as an

159

act of loving kindness to him. What a blessing he's become to me and to the church and to the community of Willow Bend — exactly what we needed! Even with all of his terrible jokes!

Long after she'd gone inside, those words from the song stayed with her, and she found herself singing them in the shower, something she always did.

It was perhaps an hour later that she called Barb.

Gracie asked, "Do you still have the music to that song we sang about friendship several months ago?"

"You mean the one starting, 'When you're lonely, need a friend' . . . ?"

"*Um-hmmm,* that's the one. What would you think about our choir's surprising Anna and Joe with that song on Sunday?"

"In church?"

Gracie heard disapproval in Barb's voice. She knew the choir director hated changing the music, once planned, so she hastened to reassure with, "I was thinking about maybe doing it during the dinner or afterward — something completely informal."

"That would be a lovely tribute! I'm sure I have the music here, so if I take it over to the church before Pat leaves — or Paul could take care of it, for that matter — copies could be run off for everyone to use at tonight's choir rehearsal."

"Great! I'll see you there."

Gracie always enjoyed choir practice, and this was an especially lively one. As a bonus, Tish had brought two of her county fair-winning apple-plum dumplings to eat afterward.

"Choir practice always gives me an appetite!" sighed Marge.

"Amen to that!" said Rick.

As for the plans to sing the friendship song, even Estelle hadn't seemed miffed that others would have parts equal to hers. Gracie thought this was a good sign — an indication that Joe and Anna inspired harmony and that the party would be one where everyone's best spirit was engaged.

Gracie told them, "This is going be a surprise for Anna and Joe and everyone else. So if anyone happens to be wearing an apron when serving, I'd suggest he or she just keep it on for the singing, too."

"I don't know if I'd go that far," Estelle stated. Nobody troubled to remind her that she wasn't one of those who usually helped much with serving.

"Since the majority of my clothing's washable these days, I seldom need to wear an apron anymore," Barb explained rather unnecessarily. "But I understand that you want us to make the tribute as natural a moment as possible." She went to the piano and got the group again intent on rehearsing Sunday morning's worship service.

They warmed up with several voice exercises, followed by the hymns Pastor Paul had chosen to go with his text and message. The anthem turned out to be somewhat difficult, but Barb insisted, "You can do it, my friends. Just push yourselves a little harder!"

There was again a small amount of grumbling about the choice. Don looked worried, and Marybeth was frowning.

"That's a lot better," Barb assured them, "but you altos were just a little late in coming in there on the middle of page three.

"First, though, I'd like to go over the bottom line on page two. Notice the change of key there, tenors. You have a two-beat rest, then come in firmly, solidly with, 'Come! The Master is calling. . . .' "

She started to play those notes again, but Lester asked her to back up a few measures, since he was still having trouble making that transition. This time the tenors were more sure of themselves.

"Fine!" Barb pronounced. "And now, everyone! We'll make a quick stab at a couple of those anthems that we'll be using during the next month or two."

A muted rustling accompanied low voices as they searched through their choir folders. Estelle sniffed as if issuing a critical comment that only she could hear. That was a change, thought Gracie. I wonder if she realizes her responses are so obvious. Then, guiltily, she added to herself, But what about my own?

"And now, Gracie," Barb said, breaking into her reverie, "would you please pass out the photocopied sheets?"

It may have been because the clock showed only a few minutes more, but that number went almost flawlessly. Once, twice, three times: They had it down cold, and all cheered as the last note died away.

It had been Marybeth's suggestion as they were enjoying Tish's treat that met with universal approval. "Look, Gracie's in charge of the dinner and will be the one to best decide the right moment for the song. Let's keep an eye on her and let Gracie indicate when that should be."

"That's okay with me." Gracie laughed. "But only if you promise not to leave me just standing there all by myself."

Marge reached out to squeeze her friend's arm. "No *way* would we let that happen, Gracie. We intend to be in on the fun, too."

163

11

Saturday had come quickly, and passed even more speedily. Gracie had spent a good part of it in the church kitchen, figuring she could get much more done there than if at home. What she hadn't considered, however, was that Uncle Miltie would insist he wanted to help, too.

Even Rocky had showed up in the early afternoon and was given an apron to protect his clothes while he chopped cabbage. "Hey, Gracie, this has to be enough already!" he griped as he dumped a mound of slaw into the large container. "I've done four loads!"

She agreed. "Then you can begin working on these carrots," she told him, sliding a couple of bags across the counter.

"Why didn't you buy those little ones that are already cleaned and ready to use?" he grumbled.

"Why, indeed?" She couldn't resist grinning at him. "Maybe I guessed that you'd be here and would need something more challenging than just opening a bag of prepared ones. Anyway, they'd be even more work to shred!"

He turned toward her uncle. "You've got to be a saint, putting up with this woman!"

"Perhaps there could be an editorial addressing the matter! Which do you think would appeal more to people: 'Saint Miltie' or 'Saint George'?"

"I suggest you stick with the first, to avoid confusion. I understand 'Saint George' has already been taken."

Gracie just shook her head as she transferred the shredded cabbage and carrots into plastic bags, ready for the refrigerator, and began making her special dressing, which would be added to it tomorrow.

Rocky had been with them for almost an hour when he got a call from one of his reporters on his cell phone. "What do you mean, Miles Stevens is going to sue?" he demanded. "Where's the information coming from?"

The other two stood there staring at him. Then Uncle Miltie whispered, "Maybe it's just a threat, just something to say." But even he looked upset. Gracie's mind was racing.

It turned out that a lawyer for Miles Stevens had just made a public statement that if the 1930-S double eagle was not returned to his client by Monday noon, legal action was going to be taken.

The clock was ticking!

Gracie had expected to pay Sally a visit on Sunday, stealing a moment between church and cooking — not late Saturday night! However, as she rather groggily reached for the phone, she found herself a moment later sitting on the edge of the bed, demanding, "What did you say?"

It was Sally. Her words were frantic. "There was someone here, demanding the coin!"

"Who was there, Sally?"

"I'm not sure who it was. I didn't really see him."

There was the sound of crying, and excited, terrified voices in the background, and Gracie asked, "Was it too dark to recognize anything that might identify him?"

"Yes. He threatened Mark. Mark tried to convince him the coin wasn't here. He refused to listen."

Gracie tried to keep her voice composed. "He left then?"

"Y-yes. None of us knew he was here till Mark woke up and found him standing over him."

"Have you called the police?"

"No-o-o! And that's what I should have done, isn't it? Instead of bothering you like this. . . ."

"Don't worry about that — but call them right now. And tell the kids not to touch anything, especially in Mark's room!"

Gracie seldom used the police chief's home phone, but now was the time for it. "It's Gracie, Herb. I just got a call from Sally, who's at this moment calling your office. There was an intruder in their house demanding the coin. He appeared in Mark's room — and it was too dark and Mark was too sleepy to recognize him."

She gave Herb what little additional information she had, then suggested, "Don't you think it's time to make public the finding of that second coin? Perhaps say that the person who can identify *that* gold coin without seeing it, giving the year and mint mark of course, might be considered as having some claim upon both of them?"

They discussed this course of action briefly before agreeing to meet at Sally's as quickly as possible.

Uncle Miltie wanted to go, too, but

Gracie asked that he stay home and call Carter, despite its being so late, to see if she'd found out anything.

"That's just an excuse not to let me go with you," he challenged through her bedroom door as she hurriedly changed back into the clothing she'd so recently taken off and left lying over the chair by her bed. "You shouldn't be going over there alone at this time of night!"

"I'll be okay, I promise." But she doubted that her smile, meant to be one of reassurance, looked any more real than it felt. "You hold the fort here, and I'll do my best there."

She gave him a brief hug on her way out the door. Every light at Sally's was on, inside and out, and all four family members were waiting in the kitchen. Kate, seven, and Jennifer, eight, were hanging onto their mother, thoroughly frightened, while Mark was indignant and upset.

After hugging Sally, Gracie asked first to use their phone. When Cordelia answered on the second ring, sounding half asleep, Gracie attempted to disguise her voice. "May I please speak to Clark Harrington?"

"Do you realize what *time* it is?" the other woman demanded.

"I'm sorry, but this is *very* important."

168

"Well!" the tourist home owner's displeasure was evident. "It had *better* be, waking up decent, law-abiding citizens like this. Hold on a minute and I'll call him."

Gracie could hear her voice, "Mr. Harrington — Mr. Harrington, you're wanted on the phone!" There was a brief pause before an even louder, more insistent, "*Mr. Harrington,* someone's on the phone, and it sounds important."

Gracie heard a banging, which she assumed to be Cordelia's pounding on his door. Then there was a pause followed by a somewhat breathless, "He doesn't seem to be here. Can I take a message?"

"No, thanks."

"He does have e-mail, you know."

She'd sounded a little more cooperative, so Gracie asked, "Can you give me his e-mail address, so I won't need to bother you?"

"Well, no . . . I don't have that, but if you leave your name and number, I'll have him call if you'd like."

"Thank you for your help, Mrs. Fountain. Perhaps I can phone him later."

"A *lot* later, you mean," the exasperated voice rejoined. "In the morning!"

Gracie rubbed her ear for a moment. "She really slammed down that receiver!"

There was a racket out on the porch. Gracie looked at the panicked expressions worn by the Canfield family. Somebody was pounding on the door and rattling the knob. And then Uncle Miltie was demanding, "Open up in there, Gracie. It's me and Rocky!"

Seeing her newest visitors, Sally asked, "What are you two doing out there at this hour?"

"Uncle Miltie called me about the problem," Rocky put in quickly, "and we decided we should be here to help. So what's happening now?"

Gracie was frowning at her uncle. "I thought you were going to call Carter."

"I did — but she'd gotten back too late and hadn't had enough time to check for you. She will tomorrow, though — I mean today," he added, glancing at the clock on the stove.

Herb arrived then. Gracie now phoned Miles's house. The phone was answered on the fifth ring. By now, if it *had* been Miles who'd so frightened this household, he'd have had plenty of opportunity to get back to his house.

"Ah, so you are home again, no?" she said in a deep voice.

"Who is this?"

She knew he was trying to identify her, and she had to be quick. "Don't do it again!" she commanded and hung up.

"What was that all about?" Uncle Miltie wanted to know.

"I — may have made a mistake on that call," she admitted.

"In what way?"

"It occurs to me Miles might be the kind of person who has caller-identification for phone calls, like we do at home."

"Oh."

Herb was looking at Gracie. "Did you tell Sally what you suggested to me?"

She shook her head. "I was waiting for you to get here."

"And we're *all* here now . . . ," Rocky smugly pointed out. "The game's afoot!"

Gracie looked startled, then recognized the allusion to Sherlock Holmes.

"We're Watson and Watson II," Uncle Miltie informed her.

Gracie now nodded at Herb. He explained that it was probably time to let word out that a second coin had been found. And that he and Gracie thought that those claiming ownership of the first coin should be obligated to put in writing what each one looked like, including specific identifying marks.

"Our printer might be able to make a change for the next edition if I get hold of him right away," Rocky immediately declared. "But what should I have put on the front page?"

"Just the basic facts, and the idea of the challenge," said Gracie. "In what you call a 'sidebar' — a boxed announcement, I think."

Uncle Miltie had gotten up a bit earlier than usual for a Sunday, so he was already sitting at the table with a bowl of cereal when Gracie appeared in the kitchen.

He tried to carry on a conversation unrelated to the events of the previous night, but as far as Gracie was concerned, what she needed once again was a little peace and quiet.

Yes, she only had one more trip out to the car with things for this afternoon's dinner.

No, she didn't need help, but thanks anyway.

Yes, they'd get to church on time.

No, it didn't seem strange at all for Anna and Joe to have this big party for everyone. As they'd said many times, they greatly appreciated the way everyone was so helpful and took them places and did things for them, and this was merely one way of saying a special thanks.

The church was full, as was Sunday school. The congregational singing of some of the old-time hymns rang forth in joy, and the choir members of the Eternal Hope Community Church didn't miss a note or a beat in their anthem, "For Love of Thee We Bring Our Praise."

Gracie had at first found herself sitting bolt-upright in the old, usually comfortable wooden chairs there in the choir loft. Then, aware of feeling more relaxed, she was able to listen attentively to Paul's sermon on "Love for a Lifetime."

She'd seen that title in the church bulletin at the beginning of the service, but it had hardly registered in her racing mind. After all, there was the dinner to finish preparing, the aftershocks from her dramatic late-night summons to the Canfields' and her curiosity about what Rocky had put on the front page of today's paper.

Hers was usually delivered before she left for church on Sunday morning. The changes to the front page must have pushed everything back.

But now, temporarily, Gracie found herself at peace, resting in the arms of God.

The kitchen was abuzz with the energy

and enthusiasm of friends who'd for years worked harmoniously together. Tish and Tyne, their houses on a different paper route from Marge and Gracie, had both read the front page, as had Eleanor McIver.

"Can you believe it, Gracie?" Eleanor was arranging chicken pieces on broiler trays. "Someone's recently found another of those gold coins. But they're not telling whether it's like the first one, or who discovered it!"

"Isn't that too much?" Tyne put in. "I'm amazed anyone could keep such a thing secret!"

"We certainly couldn't!" Tish agreed.

"I wonder if it was found out on Ferris Road, like the other one," Eleanor said. "I often drive that way, you know, and have seen different people searching around. For that matter, the whole area near where Mark found the double eagle now looks like it's been the stomping ground for a herd of elephants."

"Yeah, I've heard of elephants." That came from Uncle Miltie, who was coming into the kitchen, looking innocent except for a certain sparkle in his eyes which Gracie recognized. "A few elephants have even heard of *me*."

Tish, however, was trying to straighten out what she thought was an innocent mistake. "We were talking about the place out on Ferris Road that is all trampled down as though it was run over by a *herd* of elephants."

"Oh, *that* kind of herd." He patted her shoulder as he headed on to where Gracie was standing. "What can I help with here?"

Glancing out into the large room, she saw several of the men starting to set up tables. "It's time to get out one of those seating arrangements I saw you working on. The tables could use your supervision."

Reaching into his shirt pocket, he brought out and unfolded a sheet of paper on which were sketched two different arrangements. "I'll go over there and show them what will probably work best." He headed out of the kitchen door.

Eleanor looked quizzically at Gracie, who smiled. "It takes something like this to remind me that my uncle spent most of his career as a building contractor."

Rocky now stuck his head in the door. "So, Gracie, how did you like the layout and story in today's paper?"

When Gracie admitted she hadn't had a chance to see it yet, he went to his car for a copy.

After reading it, she told him, "My hope is that nobody new will turn up to claim that second coin." Then she added, "But it will be very interesting to see what happens!"

Sally and Mark now arrived, carrying in the huge white-frosted cake Sally had so beautifully decorated with autumnal flowers and fruits. Green vines of frosting formed the words:

WITH LOVE, PRAYERS, AND
GRATITUDE
FOR ALL THOSE WE LOVE
From: ANNA and JOE SEARFOSS,
YOUR SISTER AND BROTHER IN
CHRIST

Gracie wiped her eyes after reading the lovely sentiment, and suggested placing the cake on the corner table farthest from the entrance, at least until the official host and hostess arrived. Should they wish to have it on display somewhere else, it could then be moved.

Marge, who'd just returned, having gone home after church, commented softly, "It's a beautiful cake, but those words sound so final, as if they're leaving us."

Sally explained, "That's what they asked me to write on it, so that's what I did."

Anna and Joe soon arrived. They began greeting everyone, and expressions of mutual gratitude filled the air with each new appearance of a Willow Bend friend or neighbor.

Gracie was too busy to keep track of who arrived when. She was surprised to see that Cordelia had brought Clark Harrington with her. She went about introducing him, and, when people learned he was staying with her, he was cordially welcomed.

Sally came to tell Gracie when Miles Stevens appeared. "What do you suppose he's up to now?" Sally asked.

"I have no idea," Gracie replied. "I'd suggest that we both keep our eyes on him and on Clark."

She hadn't noticed Lynn coming toward them. But the girl was now signing something to Sally, and giving Gracie an understandable greeting of, "Hello, Mrs. Parks."

"Hello to you, Lynn," she responded slowly.

Lynn then noticed Uncle Miltie across the room and hurried over to be with him.

"Aren't they sweet together?" Sally asked. "It's a good thing I'm not jealous as her helper, for those two have bonded beautifully. She eagerly tries anything he suggests."

Added Sally, laughing, "We'd better be careful. There can no longer be private conversations when she's around — or your uncle, either, unless we turn our backs on them."

Gracie was nearly finished when Pastor Paul raised his voice above the happy hum of conversation. "Please take your places, everyone."

Gracie had no doubt that Uncle Miltie's choice as to where to sit was deliberate. He and Lynn were one table over from and facing Miles, who was seated next to Clark, of all people, at the end of their table. Sally and her daughters, being relatives-by-marriage of Anna and Joe, were at the head table, while Mark was helping to serve.

Thank goodness enough chairs had been set up for everyone. There couldn't be more than fifteen empty ones in the whole room! Paul led everyone in saying grace, then requested additional blessings upon the friendships they all shared.

Now came the infectious happy sounds of contented people eating together and thoroughly enjoying one another's company.

12

Gracie suggested that her helpers and some of the students, including Mark, now go sit with their families, at least until time for serving dessert. With so much to do and so much going on, she was too busy to pay much attention to the guests whose behavior most interested her. She did, however, touch her uncle's shoulder as she stopped to refill his coffee cup. "Everything okay here?"

He nodded so. Giving him a fast peck, she went on to the next table. When she came to Miles Stevens, she responded to his comment about her organizational skills with, "Things do seem to be going well, don't they?"

But why was he so friendly suddenly? she wondered. It didn't reassure her to know she'd find out eventually.

The phone in the kitchen rang, but by the time Gracie finished filling Clark's cup, Paul had pushed back his chair and was striding to answer it. After he had hung up he walked outside instead of returning to his seat.

A few minutes later she glanced toward the door and saw Paul coming back in, but not alone. A beautiful blonde was with him — Carter!

Setting the pot on the table, she rushed across to greet her niece with a big hug and kiss. "I'm so glad you're here!"

"I am, too! As soon as I got to the edge of Willow Bend, I tried calling your place, then here. Paul told me to come on over and eat with everyone."

"Wonderful!" Gracie wanted to ask if she had specific information concerning Clark, or if there was some other reason for coming now. But it was not the time or place for that. "Paul, how about taking her over to speak with Anna and Joe while I fill a plate with warm food from the kitchen?"

Many of Gracie's friends and neighbors knew Carter, and greeted her with friendly words. At the end of the table just before her great-uncle's, her blue-eyed, steady gaze met Clark Harrington's.

Paul said, "Carter, this is Clark Harrington, a computer and electronics expert originally from Chicago."

"Is it possible we may have met previously, Mr. Harrington? Your face seems somewhat familiar."

"No, I don't believe we have." His voice was level.

She shrugged lightly, and turned her attention toward Miles. "And I believe you are Mr. Stevens."

He actually looked shocked for a moment, before saying, "I suspect you must be Mrs. Parks's niece, from the DA's office in Chicago."

Ah-ha, he's giving Clark a warning signal! Gracie realized. What she said, however, was, "Is that an extra seat, Uncle Miltie?" indicating the one on the other side of him from Lynn.

"Afraid not, Gracie, Harry's probably coming back."

Just then Harry Durant did arrive, saying, "I've got to go. I thought I'd be back to the garage before this. With all the Sunday afternoon drivers, we get pretty busy about now."

Then, when Gracie looked across at the other table, Miles was still there — but Clark was gone!

She was distracted when Paul stood up

and presented Anna, who got to her feet, saying, "Joe and I want to thank all of you for being with us for this very special day. And I believe we also need to give a little explanation for having invited you here.

"A number of people have wondered if this marks the occasion of one anniversary or another, while others have asked — mostly indirectly, of course — if perhaps we've decided to move away or if one or both of us is sick or dying. The answer to both questions is no — at least as far as we know right now, although we're obviously not growing any younger.

"We have been to many funerals these last years, and got to talking one night about the especially large crowd who'd just come to one of those held here in our church. How pleased our late friend would have been had she been able to visit with all those people who came to bid her farewell, many of whom she hadn't seen or heard from for years.

"Well, one thing led to another, and we decided we'd much prefer having people come while we're both alive and well and capable of hugging and kissing and talking to them. But we didn't want anything real formal or fancy, or anything people would feel obligated to attend. So we decided that, if Gracie and others would take care of the cooking and serving, we'd like to have a nice sit-down, family-style meal together. . . ."

She continued speaking for a minute or two. Then Joe stood up and just said, "As always, I agree with my wonderful wife. Nothing could please us more than being here with all of you today, sharing food and the good Lord's plentiful love."

Next Paul asked if any guests would like to say a few words.

Sally Canfield reached out for the microphone and thanked Anna and Joe for all they meant to her. When she'd finished, Paul carried it to one after another of the guests. Gracie was pleased to see that Rocky was discreetly photographing each testimonial.

Paul finally said, "We are especially grateful for all of you who've so eloquently shared in words what this wonderful couple means to you. And now at the end of these public testimonies, I would like to ask the creator of this splendid feast to close with prayer."

Gracie accepted the mike, and spoke into it, at the same time beckoning to the other choir members to join her as she walked toward the head table. "Your church, your Sunday school and your choir rejoice in this time spent with you today, Anna and Joe. You have truly been trusted, special, and much-loved friends, and we honor you.

"There are so many things we would like to put into words in order to try to let you know how much you are appreciated and loved, but we'd still run out of time before they were all said. And so those of us in the choir decided to sing for you not a ballad nor timeless classic, but a simple little composition that was sung here in the church some months ago.

"Perhaps you will remember it," she said with a broad smile. "It's called 'Friendship.' Perhaps the rest of us need to hear it again more than the two of you do, but Barb is going to play the piano and we're going to sing it."

The Turner twins cleared their throats in unison while Rick Harding waggled his fingers at his giggling daughter Lillian, who sat on her mother's knee.

The group had sung the first three verses before Gracie glanced in the direction of Miles Stevens, who was looking down at the tabletop in front of him.

Then the voices of Eternal Hope's choir came to the last verse:

"Are there fences I should mend?

Broken friendships to attend?
Guide me, Lord, please lead me with Your
  hand;
For if at this life's end
I should die without a friend,
I'd be the poorest person in the land."

People applauded, but before the choir separated, Gracie picked up the microphone and bowed her head. She had an active prayer life and occasionally was asked to open or close a business or other meeting with prayer, but still this occasion was more moving than most. She closed her eyes and drew in a deep breath.

"Dear Lord, what a privilege You've given us to be here today for this blessed occasion of celebrating Anna and Joe, and what they mean to us. Thanks for letting me and others of their large circle of friends prepare this food of which we have partaken, and thanks for each one who lovingly journeyed here today at the invitation of this couple.

"But, Lord, I'm right now going to ask another blessing of You, that You will help each of us — every single one of us as we leave here today — not only to remember the love and fellowship and food, but that we are all one in You. Please help us to look around at those who may feel outside of our own little circles of friendships or family ties, and not only welcome them when they come — but invite them in, as Anna and Joe did today.

"I'm sure everyone here joins me in praying for them to enjoy many more healthy, happy, contented years, dear Lord. We ask this in the name of Your Beloved Son, Jesus. Amen."

She did not look into the face of her pastor or Carter or anyone as she hurried to the kitchen, fearing that if anyone said a word to her right then, she'd burst into tears.

13

Eleanor McIver had begun washing dishes, and several people were already drying and putting clean things away. Gracie decided she wouldn't be missed for a few moments if she went in search of her niece. But she found Rocky hurrying down the hallway toward her. "You're the one I was looking for."

"Oh?"

"We're all in Paul's office." His hand was on her elbow, though she was walking as rapidly as he was. "Your uncle and Lynn just began telling us what was said, and you need to come with me."

There in Paul's study they found Uncle Miltie trying to quote as nearly as possible the things he'd lip-read while Miles and Clark were talking to one another. Every so often he stopped to check something with Lynn.

But the girl seemed a little frustrated, causing Gracie to ask, "Would you like Sally here with us, dear?" Gracie realized that Lynn needed a surer interpreter than her struggling uncle.

A smile lit her face and she nodded. So Gracie headed out to look for her friend. She saw Mark first, and asked that he tell his mother to come to the church office right away. "Perhaps," she added, "you should plan to stay, also."

Lynn made out better in sharing her account once Sally was there. It seemed Miles Stevens had been startled to find Clark there and hadn't been pleased that the younger man was seated at his table.

Apparently Clark had been offering the older man a deal. He was prepared to get out of the picture in order to make it easier for Miles, with his local connections, to claim the coins. But Clark would do that only on condition of Miles's promising to split any proceeds evenly with him.

Miles, however, couldn't bring himself to agree to such a proposal. But he didn't exactly refuse it, either.

Carter turned to face Lynn directly. "May I ask a few questions, dear? From what you overheard, to which of the men do you think the coins might really have belonged?"

Lynn looked from Carter to Sally, and started rapidly finger-spelling. Sally listened, then asked aloud, "You are sure Clark said he knew Miles was as much of an impostor as he was, when it came to any claim to the coins?"

The child looked at them and tried to the best of her ability to say the words, "If I were Mark, I'd be very angry at people trying to take what I'd found away from me!"

"Well, I was!" Mark burst out.

"Yes, you were," his mother agreed.

"But even though the other two were making their claims and tried to appear upset, somehow they just weren't able to pull it off — they weren't angry enough," Gracie pointed out. And it was true.

Sally looked around the group. "I just want to know which of them was at our home last night."

Lynn looked very upset. Sally paid close attention. "I think it was Clark, and then Miles accused him of being a young whippersnapper!"

"How did she know how to sign 'whippersnapper?'" Uncle Miltie whispered to Gracie.

"Well, she may have been able to come up with that one, but I think the operative word is really *cahoots*. Those two, however they knew each other, were in both a tug-of-war and a conspiracy!"

Clark Harrington had been questioned by Herb, but Miles Stevens was now back in the hospital. The diagnosis this time: more heart trouble. She was pondering the issue and chastising herself for having so little sympathy for a sick man — yet, she was also having a harder time than usual feeling guilty for being judgmental.

At the deli, Abe came walking over to Rocky and Gracie after they had sat down at their favorite table. "What's your choice going to be this morning?" Gracie was keeping her thoughts about Miles Stevens to herself.

"Some tea, first of all," she told him. "And then one cookie."

"A cookie?" he repeated. "You want just one cookie?"

She nodded and sat up straighter. "Yes, dear Abe, one cookie. You can choose it."

"So, you want to live dangerously today?"

"The kind of chance I'm taking is one that puts me in the hands of someone I love. Miles Stevens and Clark Harrington took chances without honesty, without trust, without faith. Only greed drove them. And so they failed miserably at gaining what they sought. Asking for one cookie shows I'm not greedy, at least, dear Abe."

Rocky chuckled. "You find your lessons everywhere, Gracie," he said fondly.

"Well, I'd rather find lessons than coins any day. No one fights over them, for one thing. We may never know where those gold pieces came from, but what's truly golden is friendship."

And, at that moment, Abe returned and ceremoniously presented Gracie with a large piece of apple strudel.

"I didn't have a cookie worthy of you," he announced.

They all laughed.

14

Gracie over the next few days found herself worrying more about Miles Stevens's condition than she'd have expected. One thing that bothered her was that, although she had readily asked God for the banker to have a change of heart — to become the kind of person who could truly love fellow mankind, she still had to discipline herself to pray, to really pray for his well-being.

On the fourth morning, after learning of his heart attack, she finally called his stepsister. "How's Miles coming along now, Hattie?"

"I — don't rightly know. I haven't gotten over to see him yet."

Perhaps she hasn't had a way to get there since she had to give up driving, Gracie thought. "Do you need a ride? I could drive you over this afternoon, if you'd like."

"Oh, I wouldn't want to bother you."

At least she didn't say she'd rather not go. "Look, Hattie, I need to pick up a prescription refill at the pharmacy, and should stop at the grocery store for a few things. How about my coming by for you around 1:30? We'll go to the hospital and then you could come with me if there's anything you need at either of those places — or anywhere else for that matter.

"However, if you'd prefer, I could take you home before running my errands."

There was silence for an extended moment before, in a small voice, Hattie replied, "You — don't have to do that."

"It's not a matter of 'having to,' Hattie." Gracie gave a little laugh. "I'm taking the car out this afternoon, and it's no more difficult to fit two women into Fannie Mae than just one."

"Wel-l-l, I suppose. . . ."

"I'm assuming that means yes, so be ready when I arrive at half past one, okay?"

Gracie arranged miniature chrysanthemums in a small milk-glass vase to take to the hospital. *I don't know if this whole idea is what You want me doing, God, but it does feel right. I have no way of knowing whether Miles will even talk to me, or if he might command me to leave. Should that be the case, Lord, please give me the grace to not create a scene.*

I realize that he has no reason to welcome me, for I was incredibly rude to him when he called and when he came over.

Hattie carried the vase as Gracie drove, and the older woman reminisced a little. "We weren't close as children."

"What about as time went on?"

"Well, never as close as some step-brothers and -sisters. It can be a difficult relationship, sharing parents. We were practically strangers, and then suddenly we were related!" Hattie shrugged.

Gracie glanced toward her companion, who was staring out the windshield. "I'm curious. When you did see Miles in recent years, were you able to become closer?"

"Not entirely." There was another pause, which Gracie made no effort to fill.

"I think I understand," said Gracie. "Miles seems to expect to run everything his way." Hattie nodded as they turned into the hospital's parking lot. "In loving, mutual relationships there has to be give and take. Not just take!"

Even as they got out of the car and went inside the three-storied brick building, Gracie was uncertain what she should say to Miles. *Help me, Lord — please guide my tongue and my manner. Help me to do whatever You know is best.*

They rode up in the elevator. Then Gracie saw one of the physical therapists she knew walking an elderly, somewhat stooped man in hospital-issue pajamas down the hallway. She heard the hushed voice of the woman beside her asking, "That's — Miles, isn't it?"

"Yes, I'm sure it is," she agreed, and was grateful she'd made no effort to rush Hattie. They watched him enter room 209.

The therapist was encouraging him. "You did much better this afternoon, Miles." She was helping him back into bed.

He sighed heavily. Then he became aware of the two women and, holding on to the arms of the chair, he sat up straighter.

"Hello, Miles," Hattie said as she moved to the foot of his bed. "How are you feeling?"

His gaze flicked from her to Gracie, then back. "They say I'm better."

"Miles, then let's believe them!" Hattie said sharply. She looked at him. And Gracie watched them both. Neither of them is an easy person, she told herself.

Liz Eckard, the therapist, smiled at Hattie and Gracie and said, "He's coming along well." Then, turning at the doorway, she told her patient, "I'll be back in the morning. In the meantime, remember to keep doing your leg exercises."

Miles had been ignoring Gracie. Or seeming to. So she said nothing while moving the straight chair from the other side of the bed, and indicated Hattie should sit down close to him. She now set down the bouquet. "I hope you're not allergic to mums — but these are from my yard. Uncle Miltie and I thought you might enjoy them."

He nodded, just a little. "Thanks."

That didn't seem like much of a response, but she kept on talking to him. "We'd decided not to buy more varieties, but this dark pink fringe on the white blossoms looked so pretty in the catalogue that we couldn't resist."

That got little more response. "Yes. They're pretty."

She smiled at him as she sat on the side of his bed, but said nothing more for a while. Sadly, he and Hattie seemed to have little to say to one another, either. Gracie finally decided to bring up the celebration that had taken place on Sunday. "Wasn't that a lovely event? Anna and Joe have so many friends!"

Hattie now complimented her, "You

really know how to put on meals — catering them, I mean. Everything went along just as it should."

"Thanks, but I had wonderful helpers. All of the volunteers worked so well together. I could never handle all of it myself!"

"Volunteers?" Miles unexpectedly repeated. "You don't even pay them?" He sounded scornful.

"Oh, I do expect to be paid — and pay others — when it's something like a Rotary dinner or a wedding reception, but I'd never accept money for helping with something like this. After all, we're friends, and have been for decades."

Again there was silence.

Her stepbrother's taciturnity seemed to embarrass Hattie. Gracie decided to offer her the opportunity to come with her for her other errands, as she'd earlier suggested.

As Gracie followed Hattie from the room, she heard the man in the bed say faintly, "Gracie — Mrs. Parks . . ."

She turned. "What is it, Miles?"

"Would you — would you please come back to see me sometime? There are things I think — I *need* to talk to you about."

She stood there looking at him, trying to discern his motivation. *But I know, Lord, that for Miles Stevens to ask any favor is pretty difficult, so I'll take a chance.* "Yes," she said softly. "I will return — if you want me to."

"I'd — appreciate that. But next time, could it be just you? You and me?"

Hattie had walked as far as the next doorway and was standing there waiting for her, so Gracie just said, "Certainly."

Hattie asked, "What was that about?"

"He was grateful for my bringing you," she said, hoping that to be at least a partial truth. God must have some good reason for prompting her to ask Hattie to come here with her, and she assumed He must have a reason for her return.

It turned out that Hattie did need a few items at the pharmacy, and several bagsful of groceries. "I don't get to the store much," she explained. "So I take advantage of it."

Hattie didn't seem aware of the helping-hand services offered by the senior citizens task force in town. Gracie knew they could make a big difference to Hattie's life if she would only accept their outreach.

She carried most of Hattie's purchases inside her rambling old house. She'd many times admired the early Victorian exterior, which badly needed paint. Now she saw that the interior, particularly the kitchen, needed major work.

Gracie started back home, but kept

feeling nudged to return to the hospital. "I don't know why I should right now," she said out loud. But at the next street she turned around and headed back.

She walked down the hall and stopped in his doorway, wondering how to explain her presence again so soon. But Miles was still sitting where she'd left him a good two or three hours earlier. She thought she hadn't made a sound, but his head turned and, not looking surprised, he said, "Come on in."

She did so, and he went on, "I've been doing an awful lot of thinking."

"Medical crises can do that to us."

"I understand that, but there's more to what I want to tell you."

"Oh." *What can I say now, God?*

But Miles only expected her to listen, and he went on to admit that he'd been so despondent after the party that he'd considered trying to kill himself. Then the chest pains struck.

"Don't tell anyone, Gracie. It was just that — well, for the first time it hit me that if I did what Anna and Joe did, invite anyone and everyone to a party, and if you were catering that, it might very well be just you and me there. And I'd be paying you to come."

She couldn't argue that, so she just seated

herself in the chair his sister had recently vacated. "I'm sure Hattie would have come."

Suddenly the conversation took a different turn. Miles insisted to Gracie that he'd honestly thought Mark had taken his coin: It had been there on the table, then was gone. "It wasn't until days after I made that accusation that I went through everything again, all the newspapers and other stuff there in my kitchen — and it was then that I found my own double eagle.

"But I'd already told my story to everyone, and — and couldn't bear the thought of everyone laughing at me."

She sighed. "So you let everyone continue to wonder whether or not Mark was a thief."

He nodded glumly. "I was so afraid of people thinking me a fool that I decided to carry out whatever I had to do to make people believe me the victim."

"Even going to Sally's home to demand the return of the coin?"

His weary eyes opened wider. "I didn't do that. I confess to not doing what I should have, but I swear I had no part in anything like that!"

"But it wasn't Clark, either, not if what Lynn told us is correct."

"Lynn? How can that little girl tell you anything?"

He seemed genuinely to want to know, so she explained the conversation in the church office. "But what about that note on Sally's door?" Gracie waited for his reply.

She somehow believed his claim that he knew nothing about that, either and, since Clark evidently believed Miles responsible for the confrontation at Sally's, they together tried to figure out what anyone else could have to gain.

It was on the way home that Gracie put everything together and realized she needed to make one more stop, one she dreaded. *Is it really necessary for me to be the one, God? Couldn't I just go to Herb and tell him all I know — and what I surmise?*

But that feeling was still there, that urging that she must do what was right, that nobody else should be given the responsibility of accomplishing what she knew had to be taken care of.

Almost reluctantly, she made a right turn several blocks before her own home, and another one a little later. This had once been the finest part of town, where the wealthy lived in large houses with expansive lawns and enough servants to keep everything well cared for. But now the very biggest of those original mansions was a nursing home, and another had been renovated into a nonmedical residence for a number of elderly women who needed personal care.

Most had been torn down and replaced by smaller houses on smaller lots — now measured in feet instead of acres, or even fractions of these. Gracie sighed as she pulled into a driveway still somewhat protected by a not-too-stable-looking *porte cochère* that had definitely seen better days.

She turned off the engine and got out of her car, then stood there just looking around for a few moments, trying to picture what this would have been like when everything had been in excellent condition and well maintained.

Well, I'm here, Lord — and now for the hard part. She disciplined herself to walk around the car and go to the massive entrance with its two large doors and twin cast-iron knockers. She raised and lowered the one on the right, making as loud a noise as when she'd stopped there earlier in the day.

She waited for what seemed a long time before repeating her summons, and was about to press the small button set in the side of the doorway when the door was pulled open far enough for Hattie to peer through the crack before opening it a little further.

"What's wrong, Gracie? Is Miles worse?"

Gracie pushed the door open far enough to walk inside. "I need to talk with you about something, Hattie."

They were standing in the shadowy reception hall, but Hattie did not suggest their going into one of the adjoining rooms. "What did you . . . ?" But then she changed her mind and said simply, "What about?"

There were long pieces of walnut furniture with spindled arms, backs and legs — what Gracie thought of as deacon's benches — along the two sides of this space, and Gracie moved toward the one on the right. "Could we sit here for a few moments? I won't be staying long."

Hattie left the door standing open as she seated herself beside her visitor, who was saying, "I just came back from the hospital, where I talked some more with Miles."

"He is worse then, isn't he?"

"No, I don't think so, Hattie. But we did discuss matters, and now I'm wondering about several things."

Hattie shifted position. "What things?"

"Well, first of all, why did you put that note on Sally's door?"

"How did . . . I mean, what are you talking about?"

"The note you taped to their screen door,

the one that implied that Sally's a terrible person."

"Well, she *is* — she has to be! Why else would she let that son of hers get away with his thievery? Why doesn't she see to it that he gives back that coin to my brother?"

Okay, she's admitted that. Now for the major question. Gracie drew in a full breath before saying, "And that's why you disguised yourself to frighten Mark Canfield. You wanted to make them give you the coin so you could return it to him."

Hattie, eyes wide behind her glasses, reached out as though to stop her. But Gracie went right on, "You just wanted to scare them into giving up the coin."

Hattie sank back against the spindles, looking every bit her age and almost in despair. "It was all I could think of — but they wouldn't give it to me. It would have been so simple if only they'd done what I asked."

Gracie reached out to touch the other woman's arm. "They couldn't give it to you, Hattie, because they knew it was never your brother's. Mark did not steal it from him, or from anyone. He found it, just like he said."

"But Miles says . . ."

Gracie nodded. "It turns out that Miles, too, was wrong, and I'm sure he will now tell you that. He at first did think it stolen, and that's when he accused Mark — but he later discovered it had just been misplaced."

"He has it now?" Her voice quavered.

"He has it now."

"Oh, my . . ." Gracie could see Hattie was stricken.

"If you have any doubts about what I'm saying, dear, how about our calling Miles right now? He can tell you himself."

Hattie was twisting her fingers as she attempted to explain to Gracie why she had behaved so recklessly. "Miles helped me out financially a number of times when I almost lost this place. I — thought that this time I could be helping him. I really did."

"I'm sure you did."

"But I just made things worse for him and for me. And for everyone. . . ."

Gracie knew that to be true, but she said only, "However, you are now the single person who can solve the problems, Hattie. It won't be easy, but it's up to you to straighten out this situation, to put all the false accusations to rest."

It was the following morning, and Gracie and her uncle were waiting at the restaurant's door when Abe first turned his sign from CLOSED to OPEN.

"It's about time you let us in," Uncle Miltie grumbled.

Abe looked at Gracie with raised brows. "Is he always this grouchy when you get him up early?"

She laughed. "He'll calm down once he's got coffee and a bagel in his tummy."

"It'll take more than a bagel to soothe me if you're going to give me such a hard time," he protested.

"Well, we'll see what one of my fresh-from-the-oven raisin-pumpernickel bagels can do in the tranquilizer department."

Abe was chuckling as he headed around the counter, leaving these long-time patrons to seat themselves. He returned in less than a minute with a mug of coffee, a pot of tea and three of the still-warm bagels. He didn't usually have time to sit with them, but nobody else had strolled in yet. "So what's new?"

"More than you could possibly imagine!" Uncle Miltie announced, and proceeded to give a rather extensive summary of what he'd learned from Gracie.

"So Sally and Mark know?"

"Yep, Gracie took Hattie over there last night, and they got everything straightened out."

"And what about Miles? How did he take

it, finding that Hattie had gone to such extreme lengths for him?"

Gracie answered that. "Please don't tell anyone — but he cried like a baby when Hattie went back over to the hospital and told him. And she was crying even harder. They were hugging each other like they'd never stop."

Uncle Miltie explained, "They've evidently both felt lots of love for one another — but neither knew that the other felt that way, and each one was too proud and persnickety to show it."

Gracie added, "I suspect we're going to see those two doing a lot of things together from now on!"

There was a twinkle in Abe's eyes as he stated, "I want to be around when Rocky hears about this."

"But he only gets to know the mushy stuff if he promises not to print it," Uncle Miltie reminded him. "Which is like showing a starving man a — a raisin-pumpernickel bagel and telling him he can smell, but not taste it."

Her uncle looked at Gracie. "For that matter, I saw you pick up your cell phone and put it in your pocket. Let's call Rocky now and invite him for a warm bagel, my dear."

Rocky arrived within five minutes. "Wait till you hear what news I have for you!"

Uncle Miltie choked on a swallow of coffee, giving Gracie the opportunity to say, "That condition seems to be catching."

"What?" Rocky didn't get the joke.

"You go first," she said in reply, smiling at him.

So he did. His news was startling. "Clark Harrington is wanted in Wyoming and Nevada — and goodness knows where else — for illegally using his considerable knowledge of computers to run several different scams. His legitimate jobs just serve as a screen."

"So, do you think it's possible this might mean those coins just could have been his?" Abe asked, looking askance.

Gracie stared at Rocky, hardly breathing until he said reassuringly, "I doubt he'll try to claim them now. He's certainly smart enough not to want the law looking into more of his activities than they already know about."

Then he added, "Now you have to spill your beans. Time's a'wasting. The news waits for no man . . . or bagel . . . which reminds me — I'll have a poppyseed one. Make that two, with cream cheese."

Gracie read the following morning's paper before even drinking her first cup of tea. Rocky, she was pleased to see, had handled all the details involving Miles and Hattie's involvement with commendable discretion.

When she called his office, she left a message on his answering machine. "This is a brief message for an excellent editor and a truly great man. Thanks for being you, and for being my friend."

She was surprised, however, when he arrived less than a half hour later, asking, "You were pleased with the write-up?"

"Very, very much so." She had just taken from the oven a dish of stuffed French toast. "There's jam inside — do you want cherry or blackberry? I can make you a peach, if you like."

"How about one of each?"

Then, when she joined her uncle and her friend at the table, even Rocky looked thoughtful as Gracie prayed simply, "Thank You, Lord, for all the good things in life, especially for wonderful people who truly love their fellow men and try to live uprightly."

She paused for a moment before adding, "Thank You for blessing me with two such fine men sitting with me here at this table this morning." They echoed her soft amen, and Rocky reached for his fork with an expectant grin. "Boy oh boy!" he said happily.

There was fun and laughter as they finished their food. Gracie had expected to drive her uncle to the senior center, but Rocky insisted he'd do that, since it was on his way back to the office. She followed them out onto the porch, then turned to find her cat there at the door.

"I agree, Gooseberry, it's time to go for our walk. It's another beautiful day in Willow Bend, Indiana, and I feel refreshed. Come, let's enjoy it to the fullest."

She took his *meow* for an eager assent.

Gracie's Tasty Cole Slaw

√ 3 to 4 cups shredded cabbage
√ 1 carrot, finely shredded
√ 1 small onion, finely diced
√ 1/4 teaspoon dry mustard
√ 1 tablespoon lemon juice
√ 2 tablespoons tomato juice
√ 2 tablespoons corn or vegetable oil
√ 2 to 4 tablespoons mayonnaise
√ salt and pepper to taste

Mix the vegetables together in a large bowl. Stir in the other ingredients and toss well. It is important to chill the mixture well before serving.

Gracie says, "For an extra zing, sometimes I peel a Granny Smith apple and cut up half a cup of matchstick-fine slivers to throw in."

About the Author

Words have always been a joy to EILEEN M. BERGER, who learned to read at an early age and could lose herself in books and magazines, particularly fiction. Raised on a poultry farm, she spent many hours alone, feeding and watering chickens and gathering eggs. During those hours she often reimagined the plots of existing novels she had read and played with "what-ifs."

"What if the author had done such-and-such in that third chapter, *then* what would have happened?" she'd ask herself. Or, "Suppose the author's lead male had a different personality or background, *then* how would the young woman react if he did the same, or other things?" From there it was a natural step to telling herself her own stories and to promising herself to be an author someday.

But she lived for many years and through many experiences before disciplining herself to write down her thoughts, and in the meantime earned degrees from Bucknell and Temple universities — in biology, chemistry and medical technology. She became head of a pathology laboratory in a large Midwestern city before returning to Philadelphia to work toward an advanced degree. But then she fell in love with a young Baptist minister, got married and went to live in a tiny parsonage in a small north-central Pennsylvania town.

It was there, as a preacher's wife and mother, reading and telling hundreds of stories to the three little ones who soon came along, that she began writing and selling stories, poems and articles for children and adults. The books came later.

Eileen and Bob still live just outside of that same community, which they love. In addition to their church and community involvements, Eileen is active in various writers' organizations, especially the West Branch Christian Writers, the critique-support group she helped found twenty-some years ago, and is a longtime board member of St. Davids Christian Writers Association, which holds the second oldest annual conference for Christian writers in America.

The employees of Thorndike Press hope you have enjoyed this Large Print book. All our Thorndike and Wheeler Large Print titles are designed for easy reading, and all our books are made to last. Other Thorndike Press Large Print books are available at your library, through selected bookstores, or directly from us.

For information about titles, please call:

(800) 223-1244

or visit our Web site at:

www.gale.com/thorndike
www.gale.com/wheeler

To share your comments, please write:

Publisher
Thorndike Press
295 Kennedy Memorial Drive
Waterville, ME   04901